THE TWEAK

ONE SMALL CHANGE = ONE LARGE EFFECT

SUMEET S. NAVALKAR

Contents

I

It was the first day of senior college. Anant was a bit anxious. He had changed his college after the first two years, and he knew no one here in this new place. None of his friends had good enough marks to get admission to a better college. But Anant had. And so he had chosen this college. He reached college early today, before his first lecture was scheduled to begin. But as he entered the building, a student blocked his way.

"Fresher?" the student asked.

"No," Anant replied. "Senior college."

"But first year of senior college, right?"

"Yes."

"Then fresher, it is. Come with me."

"Where?" asked Anant.

"You don't dare ask questions to your seniors," said the senior student, who was still standing in front of Anant.

He got it now. This was ragging. And this senior in front of him was trying to take him away to some place away from the college staff to make him do some ridiculous things. Anant sighed. He looked small, but only because he was thin, but he was taller than average. He wore glasses that made others think he was studious. Well that, he was. But that did not mean he could not tackle such people like the one standing in front of him. He had always been aggressive. He disliked ragging. He had never done it himself, nor had he allowed himself to be ragged. This senior standing in front of him was large and would have appeared intimidating to anyone else, but not to Anant.

"Come on, now," Anant said. "I am in senior college."

"That does not stop us from having a little fun with you," the senior said.

"You think you can do that with me?" asked Anant coolly.

"Who's going to stop us? You?"

"Why not?"

The senior was a bit surprised at the attitude of this junior student. He raised his hand and brought his large right palm down on Anant's left shoulder.

"Come, we will try it out," he said to Anant.

Anant backed away a bit resulting in the slight slackening of the senior's grip on his shoulder. He then raised his left hand and grabbed the student's wrist and twisted his palm up. The next moment he caught hold of his middle finger and bent it backwards. The senior student bent his knees reflexively to relieve some pressure off his finger and staggered backwards in pain. Anant let go. Then he brought down his right hand on the student's left shoulder.

"Let's go," he said to his senior. "Otherwise your friends will think you are good for nothing."

The senior student brushed off Anant's hand and looked at him shocked.

"You think you will get away with this?" he asked.

"Sure," said Anant, smiling.

The senior gave him a 'wait till we get there' look and started walking to his right. Anant followed. The senior kept looking back at him to make sure he was indeed coming with him. Anant obliged. There was an empty corridor- empty in the sense that there was no college staff there. But there were a few students- their body language suggesting anxiety. They were queued up for their turn to get ragged. And the seniors were busy with one of them. So ridiculous- thought Anant. The juniors were more in number, and yet they were allowing themselves to be humiliated by the seniors. Anant approached the group.

"This one here is over smart," the senior student accompanying Anant told his friends.

"Is he?" another senior student, who appeared to be the leader of the group said. "He will be next then."

The leader turned his attention back to his quarry.

"Now, come on. Undress and shake your ass a bit. Let's see whether you have it in you to make a good pole dancer."

The junior shuddered.

"Do it or I will start shredding your clothes with this," the leader waved the scissors in front of the kid's eyes.

"But," the junior protested. "She is there," he pointed to the girl who was with the seniors.

"Oh, so you are shy of her? OK. She will cover her eyes, Won't you, Sheela?"

Sheela covered her eyes with her hands, keeping large gaps between her fingers through which she stared at the scared kid and smiled. The junior student looked back at the leader.

"Come on. She covered her eyes."

"No, she hasn't."

"No cheating, Sheela," the leader said and laughed, and then with his scissors, he cut off one of the loops of the kid's pants. He gasped.

"See?" the leader said. "If you delay, I will shred your clothes and then you will have to go home almost naked. Better to wiggle your ass here than to go home wiggling it in public. The junior was now almost in tears, almost resigned to his fate. Anant looked exasperated. He looked around. He saw a fire alarm. He approached it, raised his hand and brought it down with force, shattering the glass with his elbow. The corridor filled with an ear-piercing sound. The seniors looked alarmed, and started scattering. Then they realised what had happened. They knew what Anant had done. But they had to leave this place before someone arrived here. Ragging was not allowed by law, and not tolerated by the college staff. Yet it went on. The leader walked to Anant.

"I will see you later. You will pay for this," he said to Anant, brandishing his scissors in front of him.

"No, I won't," Anant said and in two quick actions, grabbed the senior student's fist that held his weapon and simultaneously pinched his nose hard, pushing his head back.

As the leader stumbled backwards, Anant extended his leg and put his foot behind the boy's foot making him lose his balance completely. As he started to fall, Anant let go of his nose and pulled his hand that held the scissors. Next moment, he grabbed the senior student's collar and turned his arm behind him. The juniors looked at Anant wide-eyed.

"You all are coming with me to the principal's office," he commanded. "And you will be making an official complaint."

The other seniors were no longer in the corridor. They had escaped before they knew what had happened to their leader.

"Sheela!" the leader called as he was shoved by Anant towards the principal's office.

"No one's coming for you. Now walk straight, or I will break your arm," Anant shouted over the shrieking alarm, as a security guard came running to see what had happened.

After Sheela's name was disclosed in the principal's office, the leader of the ragging group vomited out the names of his accomplices, and all of them along with Sheela and the boy who had blocked Anant's way, got suspended.

Anant was twenty minutes late for his first lecture. But the professor took him in looking at his innocent looks. Anant settled down on the first empty seat that he found in the classroom, in a bid not to distract the class more than he already had. The lecture ended twenty minutes later.

"Hi," he said to the girl, beside whom he had taken his seat. "Sorry, I came in late. So I took this seat. Will anyone be occupying this seat? Should I find some other place?"

"No. It's OK. I don't have any friends here," the girl replied. "I am new to this college."

"Me too. I am Anant."

"I am Pooja."

And then their conversation ended, as a new professor entered the classroom.

After the lecture, they had a break of half an hour.

"I am going to the canteen," Pooja declared.

"May I join you?" Anant asked.

It had been a week now since college started, and Anant and Pooja had not made any friends. For them, the other students were just classmates. But they thought of each other as friends. It was a friendship built out of necessity for company. They were both outsiders in this college and coincidentally, they had happened to meet each other right on the first day in the first lecture; this had brought them closer. By the second week, they both had started bunking lectures that they thought were boring, but having opted for science, they couldn't bunk the practicals. They were important. For the rest of their studies involving theory, they both preferred the books over their professors. So, they went to the library together, were together during their breaks and also did the experiments by each other's side.

Pooja Sathe came from a family with a background in science. Her father worked as a real scientist in a private institute. Anant Godbole looked at her with envy when she told him about her father. Anant came from a lower middle class family with not much of a background in science or for that matter, in education. But his parents had always been very supportive of his educational aspirations.

As time passed, both Pooja and Anant started being friends with other students as well. This, though gave them less time with each other, they saw to it that their friendship remained unaffected. It was no longer a friendship born out of necessity for company. They now knew that they missed each other when they were with their other friends. Most students thought of them as a couple, but they totally denied having any romantic feelings for each other.

"They think we are a couple," Pooja once said to Anant; they were sitting in the library.

"Yes, I know. And the first time I heard it, it gave me butterflies in my stomach."

"What?"

"Yes, I was excited to hear that they thought I had a girlfriend. But don't you worry. That was just a passing feeling, and it wasn't about you, but about the idea of me having a girlfriend."

"Oh! Then it's fine. So? What should we do about that- about them thinking...?"

"Nothing," Anant replied. "Do we need to do something?"

"No. I just asked..."

"But why don't you have a boyfriend?"

"Never thought about it. And what about you?"

"I am straight. I don't want a boyfriend."

"Shut up! Why don't you have a girlfriend? You are quite neat. And you look all nice and cute and innocent. Girls like you. One of my friends asked me if I am not involved with you, then could she..."

"Who?" Anant suddenly felt interested.

"Hahahaha... Your butterflies came back?"

"Obviously. Who is she?"

"I won't tell you. She told me specifically not to tell anyone about it."

"Come on, now. You will be doing her a favour. If I feel interested in her, I may just ask her for a date, and she will be in fact happy that you told me about her."

"But if you were to like her, you would have already liked her. If I tell you about her and then you start liking her, it would just be your butterflies, nothing else, nothing real."

"Correct and wrong. I agree that I may start liking her when you tell me she's interested in me, but that does not mean it would just be butterflies and not something real. You remember how we became friends. We used to be with each other only because we didn't have anyone else to be with. But then we became real friends."

"OK. Fine. She is..."

Some other place: Some other time:

Krishna was in his first year as a professor. This was his first job. He was young, but not the youngest of the teaching staff- something that would have made him prouder. There was another professor who was younger than him, and he resented her. Well, the resentment was not because she had managed to acquire professorship one whole year earlier than Krishna, but because she was a person to be resented. She was a haughty woman. She was bookwormish- intelligent but bookwormish- in the sense that, as Krishna had observed, she rarely thought out of the box. And yet, Lalita was arrogant... about what, thought Krishna.

"There couldn't have been life on Mars. Never," Lalita was saying to one of her colleagues.

"Why do you think so?" asked Krishna as he settled down in the staff room.

"Because Mars has silicon. Much more silicon than our Earth has. And silicon is poison."

"Poison to life forms like us, maybe. Humans or life on earth may not thrive on Mars, but that does not mean..."

"But carbon is the base of all life," she stated matter-of-factly.

"Silicon also, like carbon, has a valency of 4," Krishna argued. "That means silicon, like carbon, can form bonds with four other atoms and if carbon-based life forms can exist, so can silicon-based, I think."

"There is no proof for that," Lalita said stubbornly, "that silicon-based life forms can exist."

Krishna knew Lalita had lost the argument. She could not refute him. She had started the topic with a speculation- that life on Mars could not have been possible, and yet she now needed proof for Krishna's speculation. He smiled pleasantly at her, and opened his lunch box. He placed the opened lunch box on a newspaper when he noticed Professor Supriya looking at him. She smiled at him, acknowledging she had been listening to his debate with Lalita. He smiled back. He had never spoken to Supriya- at least not in a conversation. There was an occasional 'hello' or a smile while passing through the college campus, but nothing else. Both used to get nervous in each other's presence, and would always manage walking away in opposite directions quite quickly. They were aware of the sexual tension between them. She thought of him as extremely handsome, and he thought she could have been a model. They both knew that they could, if they wanted to, overcome their nervousness and talk, but neither had done it. She was his senior and a good three years older than him. Not that it mattered to them, but if ever they were to progress to a romantic relationship, their affair would be frowned upon. Societal pressures. Krishna would have taken on the society, but he wasn't sure Supriya could and would. And so Krishna and Supriya only shared self-conscious smiles with each other. Supriya's department was Chemistry. Krishna's department, as was Lalita's, was Biology. So Krishna also couldn't have found some good excuses to go and talk to Supriya. Not that the staff from different departments did not intermingle, but when the sexual tension was so tangible, excuses didn't seem to come by naturally. Krishna could manage to go and talk to anyone from a non-science department, but not so with Supriya. And Supriya too had these same deterrents acting for her as far as Krishna was concerned.

Towards the end of the second term, Krishna and Lalita one day were working in the biology laboratory, working on some experiment that always took long to finish. One by one, all the students had left after performing their experiments, leaving only the two of them in each other's company. Their day was still long from over. They had kept the centrifuge running, and now they sat down at a table, reading. Neither of them liked talking to each other. The centrifuge had to be run for not less than two hours. Krishna slumped lower into his chair, and didn't realise when he dozed off. Lalita looked at him disapprovingly, and continued reading her book. But the disapproving look didn't mean much, for after a few minutes, she too lowered her head on the table, and went off to sleep. There was silence in the laboratory, except for the low humming of the centrifuge.

Anant and Pooja:

Anant was eyeing Pooja. She had still not told him who her friend was- the friend who was interested in him.

"Complete the sentence, Pooja," Anant pleaded. "You almost said her name."

"Yes, but I have second thoughts about it," Pooja said.

"But why?"

"It doesn't seem right to divulge her secret."

"I am not going to talk to her if I think I am not interested in her. Moreover, it's not like I will go and tell anyone about it."

"Would you have told me if a boy had asked you about me?" Pooja asked.

"Hmmm.... In fact, most boys think you are too intelligent for them and so they stay away from you."

"What? This is ridiculous. So being intelligent is why I still don't have a boyfriend."

"But I don't think so."

"What? You don't think I am intelligent?"

"No. I meant that shouldn't be the reason for them to stay away from you."

"OK. So you in their place would have...?"

"Yes. Sure. But now tell me who that friend of yours is."

"OK. But promise me..."

"I promise," Anant said in a hurry.

"Tejaswini."

"That hot girl?!"

"Shut up, Anant."

"What, shut up? She is hot."

"Don't say that."

"OK. I won't say it, but that doesn't stop me from thinking that she is..."

"OK. Think whatever. I am leaving."

"What's wrong with you?"

"Nothing. I just don't like you saying that about Tejaswini, or for that matter about any girl..."

"Jealous?" Anant teased.

"Why would I be jeal...?" Pooja stopped talking, her eyes looking distantly, as if she was thinking. "That can't be... I *am* jealous, Anant."

She suddenly stood up and stormed out of the library. Anant gathered his book, stuffed it inside his bag and ran after her. As he did so, he realised how much he cared for Pooja. She had become his dearest friend.

"Wait," Anant called after Pooja who had just reached the stairs.

She stopped for a moment, but then she started descending the stairs again. But he now caught up with her.

"Why are you jealous?" he asked.

"Don't ask questions, answers for which are so obvious," she scolded him.

"It is nothing obvious. Now stop, will you?"

Pooja stopped.

"Why are you jealous?" he asked again.

"Why do you think I am?"

"OK. Let me enumerate the possible reasons for you. You are my friend, and naturally you feel a bit possessive about me. If I have a girlfriend, we may start not being with each other as often as we are right now, and that can make you jealous about my currently non-existing girlfriend. Second possibility is that when we have been such good friends, how could I think of some other girl and not you? That is, how could I find some other girl attractive even when you are persistently in front of me? Again, this is a natural thought. You are a girl and when one of your friends finds some other girl attractive, you may wonder what's wrong with you that you were overlooked. Third possibility is the combination of the first two possibilities. And there is also a fourth possibility that you have fallen in love with me."

"Finally!" Pooja exclaimed.

"What finally? Do you mean to say that you have fallen in..."

"Yes. Isn't that obvious?"

"No, it is not," said Anant. "That's why I enumerated the possibilities of why you might have been jealous."

"When you said Tejaswini is hot, I couldn't take it. And I won't be able to take it if you think those things for any other girl too. And that's because somewhere in my mind, I want you to feel those things for me."

"Are you sure? Because, from my perspective, I feel that you are just possessive about me."

"And why would I be possessive about you?"

"Because I am your friend," said Anant.

"I am possessive about you because I love you, Anant," Pooja said, and realised that she had just said it.

Anant couldn't say anything. Pooja had also fallen silent.

"Well then...," she said, "I know that you don't feel the same for me."

"You don't know that."

"What do you mean?"

"I mean I have not said anything yet. So don't start assuming. But I seriously feel you have confused some other feelings for love."

"See? You are just denying that I might have actually fallen in love with you, and that's because you do not feel it for me," she reasoned.

"Do you want to kiss me?"

"What?" Pooja was shocked. "All boys just jump at any chance they..."

"No, I didn't mean that. I asked because I am not sure that you have deciphered your feelings correctly. I asked because if you don't feel like kissing me then probably I am right and that you just misunderstand..."

But Anant could not complete what he was saying, for Pooja suddenly dropped her bag and kissed him on his lips. Anant's brain went completely blank. She stopped for a moment, but only for a moment, and then she continued as if she could not stop herself. As far as he was concerned, his body had completely gone numb, for all his attention was on his own lips being kissed by Pooja's soft lips. He let his mind bathe in this sensation for a few moments and then he kissed her back. Then he suddenly pushed her away realising that they were in the college. He looked around expecting someone would have already seen them kissing, but this part of the college was completely empty. It was just outside the library, and it was meant to be empty anyway. Anant placed his hands on Pooja's waist, pulling her close, and then he kissed her again.

A few moments later, they had let go of each other and each other's lips. Pooja stood embarrassed as Anant bent down to grab her bag which she had hastily thrown away in her moments of her passion. He handed her the bag, which she took without looking at him. He started descending the steps slowly; she followed. Neither spoke until the time they were outside the college.

"Now, are you sure," she asked, "that I am in love with you?"

"Huh? Yes. But..."

"But you are not sure whether you want me as your girlfriend, and I understand. And don't let that kiss make your decision for you."

Anant didn't say anything. He knew she was one of the closest friends he ever had. He liked her and he cared for her. He didn't want her to get hurt. And now, after that kiss, Pooja seemed hot too. At this thought, he subconsciously took a step back from her to look at her. She had a sweet round face, a short nose, chubby cheeks, thin delicate lips- his eyes lingered on her lips for a few moments, and then his gaze darted downwards at her body. Indeed she was hot. Her body was as hot as Tejaswini's, but then why hadn't he noticed this earlier? Maybe because he had always thought of Pooja as his friend and not explicitly as a girl. Or maybe it had to do something with her face. She looked sweet, and for Anant sweet and hot didn't seem compatible. But now, at this moment for him, sweet and hot had reconciled.

"Stop staring at me like that," she said, barely opening her mouth.

"In fact, I was ogling...," he said. "Why didn't I notice this sexy body before?"

"That's why I told you; don't let that kiss decide it for you. At this moment, you will find me sexier than the sexiest woman in the world. Go home. Don't think about the kiss. Only then you can decide a bit logically. And remember that I don't expect anything from you. I am ready to forget the last fifteen minutes or so completely for the sake of our friendship."

But Anant knew better; they probably would not be able to remain friends if he rejected her.

Biology Laboratory: Krishna and Lalita:

The soft hum from the centrifuge continued as if singing a lullaby to the occupants in the room, who slept soundly waiting for the machine to run for the stipulated time, waiting for the lullaby to stop. Sometime while Krishna and Lalita were sound asleep, a security guard had come up from the ground floor to lock all the classrooms. He checked every classroom and after ensuring that no one was there, he closed and locked the doors. Same was going to be the case with the biology laboratory. He opened the door of the laboratory. The lights were on. But that was usually the case. Some students saw to it they switched off the lights if they were the last ones to leave; some students didn't care. Assuming that no one had bothered to switch off the lights, the security guard switched off the lights. But again, he glanced across the laboratory. He saw no one. Krishna had slumped down in his chair and Lalita had placed her head on the table. The guard did not see anyone as the high laboratory platforms on which the students performed their experiments blocked a clear view of the low table at which the professors sat. The guard went out, closed the door and locked it.

The lullaby stopped. The centrifuge had beeped. Krishna stretched his legs and opened his eyes. It was dark; it was already past dusk. He went and switched on the lights. It was good that someone had thought of saving electricity and switched off the lights- probably Lalita. She was still asleep. He knocked on the table to wake her up. She opened her eyes and looked at Krishna, disoriented. Her eyes widened; she kind of looked shocked to see him in front of her. He guessed what she was thinking.

"You are not at home; we are still in the laboratory," he said and smiled.

"Oh! Oh yes!"

Lalita washed her face and walked towards the centrifuge. Krishna had already taken out the tubes from the machine.

"Let's finish this off," he said.

In around an hour, they had completed the experiment. They put their belongings in their bags and started towards the door. Lalita grabbed at the handle and pulled as Krishna started switching off the lights. She gasped. He looked at her.

"They have locked us in," she said, her eyes going wild.

And then suddenly, she started banging on the door, desperately. Banging, pulling, pushing, and shouting. Krishna switched back on the lights that he had switched off, and went back to the table and placed his bag on it. He then opened the windows. The nearest building was far off. Moreover, the windows of the laboratory were protected by a grill to ward off birds. He looked down. There was a road below- he knew- but it wasn't visible from any of the windows. He looked out the windows on the other side. No luck. Lalita was still desperately trying to unlock the door, which Krishna found totally a waste of time and energy. She had shouted and yelled for quite some time now and if no one had responded, he knew, no one was able to hear her. He sat back at the table, quite coolly.

"Do something," Lalita said. "How can you go and sit there when I am struggling to get us out."

"Thank you, Lalita, for doing what you could. I would have done the same thing if you hadn't, but not for this long. And while you were busy there, I looked out of the windows, but I don't think anyone will be helping us tonight. Better come and sit here and relax."

"You know what this means?" she asked, looking incredulously at him.

"We are locked here for the night."

"Without any food or water."

"Food, yes- we don't have any. But we can drink water from the taps, and we have ethanol or ethyl alcohol if we need to get high."

"Have you lost your mind? There is no toilet in the laboratory."

"Uh-oh," Krishna had not thought about it.

"And I have to relieve my bladder. NOW!"

"Oops," Krishna said. "Cool down first. Going all mad is not going to help. Accept the fact that we are locked in for the night."

Lalita looked at him, but she thought about it, breathed in deeply, and came and sat in front of him.

"Now what?" she asked, expectantly.

"You need to urinate," he said and she winced at the crude use of his words- for he didn't believe using some euphemism like emptying the bladder instead of the word 'urinate' was going to improve Lalita's situation.

"Yes," she said. "And to remind you- I am a woman. I can't do it in an empty bottle like you men."

Krishna smiled, but it was an embarrassed smile.

"But," he said, "adding to the idea of using a bottle- you can do it in a bucket. Can't you?"

Lalita considered.

"We have a small bucket there in the storeroom," he said, pointing to a small room with a door which stored all the apparatus that was required for the experiments. "You can go in, relieve yourself, then bring out the bucket and pour its contents into the sink here. As I said, we have ethanol and we also happen to have phenol and phenyl also."

Lalita seemed to have cooled down. She did as Krishna had suggested. She went into the small room and closed the door. He heard the plastic bucket being placed on the floor, and then a muffled sound of liquid being poured into the bucket. She couldn't shut that sound in. Poor woman, he thought. But if he had to do that- and he shuddered at the thought of using that same bucket- that sound was probably going to be much louder. Or perhaps not, he thought, as he imagined what he would do. By the time she came out of the storeroom, Krishna was ready with the phenol and ethanol bottles. She clumsily held the bucket away from his line of sight.

"You don't look here. Close your eyes and face the wall."

"Is that a punishment right from school books?"

"Krishna, please do as I say," she almost screamed.

"OK. OK. Don't get all excited. We don't want you to splash the contents out now, do we?" he said and laughed, and then closed his eyes and looked away.

She was irritated, but at the same time, she couldn't help smiling at what he had just said. And she was relieved to see that he had looked away before her face had broken into a smile; she didn't want him to see her smiling at his joke.

"Good it was your bladder," he said, while she emptied the contents of the bucket into the sink, "and not your rectum that needed the emptying. Imagine the mess..."

She closed her eyes and winced again, getting angrier, but at the same time, she couldn't help smiling at his joke again. She didn't say anything, but glanced at him, and was grateful to find him still looking away. Twice!- she thought. Twice- in the last few minutes, he had made her wince and twice, he had made her smile. She glanced at him again; he was still facing away. He was decent; she knew. But at the same time, he kept saying things that no decent man would say, and she knew it was only to irritate her or to embarrass her.

"OK. Done," she said.

"Fine," he said, getting up and approaching her. "Now, my turn."

Lalita instinctively backed away, holding the bucket behind her.

"You are not using the same bucket," she glared at him.

"We have only one bucket."

"Whatever, but you are NOT..."

"You don't really expect me to do it in a bottle, do you?"

"Why not?"

"Lalita, what if it gets stuck?"

Lalita's jaw fell open as Krishna caught hold of the bail of the bucket behind her and snatched it away, and then went into the storeroom. She shook her head as she recovered from what he had just said, and then again-for the third time now- she winced and smiled at almost the same time.

Lalita waited for him at the table, and when he came out of the storeroom, she looked away. He smiled looking at her. Circumstances had forced them to be with each other and they were forcing them to talk as well. And for the time being, he was enjoying shocking her with his comments. After he got the bucket and the sink cleaned, he went and joined her at the table.

"You are intelligent, Lalita. I know that as a fact. But you don't apply your intelligence. That's why I don't talk to you much."

"Wow. Why this sudden candour?"

"And you are arrogant too."

"And now you are back with your insults," she said and rolled her eyes. "What did I ever do to you?"

"Nothing. I just don't like your arrogance."

"And now- candour and insult combined. Why are you being rude?"

"Sorry. I know that sounds rude but I was just being frank, and making some conversation."

"Your idea of conversation is revolting."

Krishna smiled.

"You have the ability to insult a person too," he said, "but that ability of yours comes from your arrogance."

"And what does your ability to insult come from?" she asked.

"Same source- your arrogance. Have you ever seen me insulting anyone except you?" he asked.

"You can say such things without even a modicum of emotion," she said. "Someone who does not know the language in which we speak, may really feel you are making a very friendly conversation."

"No, really. I am making a friendly conversation. Trust me. I respect your intelligence, your knowledge, your sincerity in your job. Perhaps you are the only professor in our college who will manage this year to complete the syllabus she was assigned to teach. I am sincere too, but I am still far behind and I don't think I can manage to complete it now. The thing that I don't like in you is your arrogance."

"OK. Fine. You said it loud and clear that you don't like me," Lalita said. "But I don't want you to like me. I am better off not talking to rude people like you. And I reciprocate your feelings. I don't like you either."

"But I like you."

"What?" she exclaimed.

"Yes, I find you irritating because of your attitude, and as I said you don't apply your knowledge well. That part bothers me because you are intelligent and yet you stick only to the syllabus and the textbooks. Apart from these two things I find you are a fine person. In fact, I envy you. You are the youngest professor in our college."

Lalita felt a bit uncomfortable with some praise coming from Krishna.

"We should have had a phone line here. There should be one in each laboratory," Lalita said, trying to change the subject.

"Oh, you got uncomfortable?" he smiled. "That's a likable characteristic in you."

"Now, you are purposely making me more uncomfortable. But you should know that arrogance- if you want to call it that- is in my nature. I can't change my nature. And I am not arrogant with people who I consider my friends."

Krishna smiled.

"By the way," he said, "we have a phone just behind that wall, in the next room. Had we been locked in there, we would have been able to call someone to let us out."

"I am going to make an official complaint about that guard. How could he...?"

"I don't blame him. He has to close all the classrooms. And I have seen him look inside each room before he closes it. He must have done it here too. You had your head on the table and I was sitting quite low in my chair, and he mustn't have seen either of us. I don't think he locked us in without checking. And all the lights were switched off here when I woke up. Unless you did that, I reckon he had a look in this room before locking it."

"Oh. OK. I won't make a complaint then. Now, I see why you say I don't apply my intelligence and knowledge."

"No," Krishna said, "this time you weren't aware that the lights were switched off, and from your point of view, you were right."

"When you say anything good about me, it is so rare that it seems like you are flirting."

"Oooooh nooooooo, me flirting with you? Now, that..."

"Don't say anything insulting please again. It hurts," Lalita said.

Krishna's face suddenly became strained and serious. He didn't say anything. He thought about it and realised that he indeed had been hurting her.

"I am very sorry," he said. "I mean it. Extremely sorry. I always thought you were arrogant, and I took it personally. Well, that's my nature. I can't tolerate arrogance- my flawed nature. As you said and you are right- you never did anything to ruffle me personally, but I was a lot irritating to you, like that day when I interfered when you were talking about Mars to your friend. I shouldn't have, and now I realise my mistake. I am sorry for being so obnoxious to you when you never gave me a reason to do so. I always thought you were the villain between the two of us, but now I realise I was the one who always behaved badly with you, and in doing so, I was wrong."

Lalita smiled a faint smile.

"You can be nice," she said.

"No, not nice. It's just regret. I did exactly those things to you I hate to see in other people. I really don't know how I am ever going to make up for all those wrongs."

"It's OK, Krishna. I know I am arrogant. But now I think I can no longer be arrogant with you."

"And I will never be rude or insulting to you again," he said and smiled awkwardly.

"Now, let's talk about something else," she said.

"Yes. If I don't insult you, you think I am being a flirt, right?" he smiled.

She smiled too, and then suddenly her smile faded away.

"What happened? Did I say anything wrong again? I didn't mean to," Krishna looked tense.

"No," she said. "I just realised how people will react to this. The two of us-locked up here for an entire night!"

"Oh, don't even think about people. They will gossip even when there is nothing to gossip about."

"That's easy for you to say. You are a man. I am a woman."

"There is no difference between a man and a woman."

"I know that, but people... You will get away with it. I won't."

Krishna opened his mouth to say something, but he stopped. He knew she was right. A girl alone with a man all night. That was not going to be easy for her. He had never cared for people, but Lalita did care, and she was not wrong in doing so. He had all the logical arguments, but he didn't know how he was going to convince her that it didn't matter because it did matter. People would forget him, but they would remember her as the one who was alone with...

"What am I going to do?" she said, her face buried in her hands.

"You know," he said, trying to make a conversation, but not knowing exactly what to say, "there is nothing wrong with sex." (At this, she looked up at him.) "It gives pleasure. I don't understand why there is such taboo surrounding it. A man and a woman have sex. What's wrong about that? It's natural."

"No, it's not natural if they are not married at the time," she argued.

"Come on. A lion and a lioness are not married when they have sex or even at the time they have cubs."

"We are not animals."

"We are animals," he said emphatically. "And of all people, you should know that; you are a biologist."

"But we are intelligent animals."

"And yet we are so foolish to consider something as natural as sex a taboo. Logically, what is wrong in two people giving pleasure to or seeking it from each other?"

"We live in a society which has made some rules..."

"Rules on the basis of what? Rules should be logical. I see those rules only as some random organised set of stupidity, made because someone sometime thought it wise to impose his thoughts on others."

"But sex without commitment..."

"...is still pleasure," Krishna completed Lalita's sentence.

"But what about the child that is born out of such a relationship? If the man is not committed, he won't strive to support the child and the entire responsibility would be on the mother."

"OK. I have to agree to this. Now, I understand why sex without marriage was considered wrong in the old times in the light of what you said about children born out of such relationships, but in modern times, this has become obsolete. How would a child be born if we use protection? But even if such an accident happens, abortion is legal in our country, is it not? Unlike many countries that proclaim themselves to be developed and progressive and then strip a woman of her right to bear a baby or not on the basis of religious beliefs, our country is far better on this front. Abortion is legal, and I don't think you should say anything against that law because as you said society makes some rules, and they need to be followed, right? Now, if abortion is legal and contraceptives are legal, then how can a relationship of sex between a man and a woman be frowned upon? Society contradicts its own rules. That's why those rules are illogical. And those rules are not even legal. You cannot be jailed for having sex with a man before marriage or before you are committed to him."

"But ethics..."

"Ethics?" Krishna scoffed at that word. "Ethics are different in different cultures. What is supposed to be ethical in one society is unethical for another and vice versa."

Lalita didn't say anything. She could not refute Krishna logically. And Krishna didn't seem to be of those types who would listen to anything short of reason.

"Now," Krishna said after a few minutes of silence, "look at our situation. You sit there wondering what people will think because we were alone here for the entire night. In reality, nothing happened between us. Yet people will assume that something happened. Why can't they assume that nothing happened instead of assuming that it happened? What's the logic in such assumptions? Those assumptions are made because society also knows that it's natural to have sex, and if it is natural, then there is a higher probability that it happened than not. And if it is natural, then my point is what's wrong about sex? But at that point, people stop thinking logically and stick to rules that they don't realise were imposed upon them- rules which do not come to them naturally- rules which deep down they want to break themselves, but they don't for the fear of their own selves. The best part is some of us don't even realise that we want to break those rules. This is all bullsh... ...My question is that if as it is, people are going to assume that we had sex tonight, then why not have sex and at least give each other some pleasure?"

Lalita gasped.

"What are you saying?" she said, alarmed and suddenly sat up straight in her chair, which was actually her bid to back away from Krishna.

"Oh. Cool down," said Krishna. "I didn't realise how it would sound to you until I said it. I didn't mean us in the Lalita and Krishna sense. I meant any two people like us who may happen to be in a situation like we are in at this moment."

"But we are in that situation, and you suggested sex as a pass-time. So it applies to us as well. And if so, you suggested that you and I have sex. You are not at all decent as I thought you were," Lalita said, still looking alarmed.

"Wait, wait," Krishna said. "I don't regret saying there is nothing unethical about sex before marriage or even without committment, but trust me; I have no intention of having sex with you. Though I said I was wrong in how I have treated you until now, and though I don't think of you now as the repulsive person I thought you were till just a few hours back, that does not mean I have become so fond of you as to entertain the idea of having sex with you. It wouldn't be pleasurable for me."

At this, Lalita totally believed him- believed that he hadn't suggested they have sex. An insult- he had just insulted her again, but this time, he didn't do it intentionally. Perhaps, he didn't realise it even now after saying it aloud that he had insulted her. She shook her head and smiled sadly. But something tugged at her mind. This man here had just made her feel that she was ugly- not really- he hadn't said it, but whatever he had said had made her feel that he didn't think of her as a woman- a woman sexy enough- a woman, woman enough. Wasn't she a woman who a man would desire?

"Why did you smile?" Krishna asked.

"Nothing," she said, but it wasn't nothing.

How dare he not think of me as a desirable woman?- this thought boiled inside her, and then she suddenly stood up, and walked across the table to Krishna. He was sitting with his hands on the table. She looked down at him, and then she sat on the table, and shifted so that her hips brushed against his fingers. He quickly pulled his hand away. He looked at her with a confused expression. She smiled- a lop-sided sensuous smile. He blinked. And then she raised her hand and touched his cheek, a faint smile still visible on her face. Now, he was alarmed, but he didn't push her hand away. Encouraged, she moved her fingers up and down his cheek. He stopped breathing, and every muscle in his body went rigid as a tingling wave originating in his cheek travelled through his body. She moved her fingers down to his neck and then towards his chest. He swallowed. He didn't move, but suddenly he had started breathing again and she could feel his ragged breaths on her hand. And then she smiled broadly and stopped, pulling her hand away. She stood up again and went back to her chair.

"What was that for?" Krishna asked after his body relaxed.

"What did you say? Sex with me wouldn't be pleasurable for you? You insulted me again. Did you realise that?" she said, but her voice wasn't angry.

"Sorry. I didn't mean to insult you."

"I know you didn't mean to insult me."

"So you did all that just to prove me wrong?"

"No. I did it to see whether I was a desirable woman."

"And?"

"And I think I am," she said, smiling.

"What if I had lost control?"

"You *had* lost control."

"Yes, but not totally."

"I was sure you wouldn't," she said with an impish expression on her face.

"You... you... are...," he seemed lost for words.

"Arrogant? I know," she grinned.

III

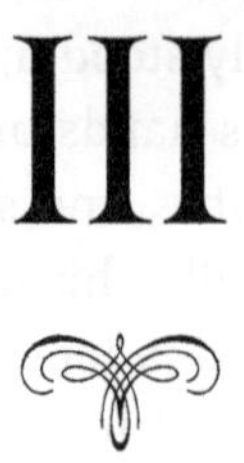

Anant:

While travelling home, Anant's reality was blurred. There was basically nothing going on in his mind, and he knew something ought to go on. He had just kissed a girl- well, kissed her after she had kissed him, but that was not the point. It was his first kiss- that was what it was, and at the moment, it was as if there were no thoughts in his brain. Perhaps he was overwhelmed by what had happened, and it was not just the kiss, but also the fact that he was under pressure to think about Pooja- whether he wanted her to be his girlfriend or not. He felt no pressure though at this moment. Everything seemed distant to him. When he reached home, he just jumped up in his bed, lay down and closed his eyes.

"Not feeling well?" his mother asked.

"No, I am fine. Just tired."

When he thought of the day's events, Anant felt a wave of excitement run through him. Today, he came to know that two girls were interested in him. The kiss with Pooja had overshadowed what she had told him about Tejaswini. Anant had always eyed Tejaswini up from a distance. Though he was attracted to her, he had never even thought of approaching her. She was a glamourous kind of a girl, and Anant had never thought a girl like her would even look at him twice. Though the glamourous type, she never came across as haughty or reserved. She appeared friendly and he liked that quality in her. And this girl- who he had thought wasn't even aware of him- was actually interested in him! Wow, he thought. But he didn't know her, and on the other hand, he knew Pooja quite well. Pooja was his closest friend, and he liked her. And it was only because of her that he had come to know about Tejaswini's attraction for him. Well, he might have come to know about it one day or the other. Hmmm... perhaps, perhaps not. What if he had not known about Tejaswini? Then, would he have accepted Pooja as his girlfriend? Yes. He had never thought of her romantically, but after knowing she was interested in him, he would not have rejected her. And so, it was decided. But was this the effect of her kiss? Most probably not. Kiss or no kiss, he could not reject his close friend.

The next day, Anant, before he could want to change his decision, went to look for Pooja, and as he entered the corridor outside the classrooms, he saw her walking just in front of him. He tapped her shoulder. She turned.

"Hi," she said, and smiled.

"Hi," he waited for her to ask him what his decision was, but she didn't; so he asked, "Have you changed your mind?"

"About?"

"How can you ask that?" he said.

"I want to be sure what you are referring to."

"Now, are you sure?"

"Yes," she smiled shyly, "and no, I haven't changed my mind. I am sure about what I feel for you."

"You didn't even know about that till yesterday morning, and in one fleeting moment of jealousy, you became so confident?"

"Yes, I realised it. But I would have thought more about it later on. But then your idea of the kiss- well that- helped me ascertain. When you asked, I was shocked, but the next moment I knew that I wanted to do it."

"And you did it without taking my permission?"

"Sorry for that, but I think you would have liked to kiss any girl. So me kissing you was good for you, wasn't it?"

"What? What are you saying...?"

"Stop acting. Boys are quite indiscriminate when it comes to..."

"You think...?"

"I am sure. Just imagine someone else in my place yesterday. What would your reaction be?"

The first name who Anant thought of was Tejaswini. But he didn't imagine her kissing him. He immediately discarded the thought, because obviously he would have liked it. He should think of someone else. Hmmm... Vidya? Well, yes. Pratishtha? Maybe her too. Priya? Leela? Oops.... Pooja seemed to be right. He wouldn't have minded a kiss from any one of them. Or for that matter from anyone else.

"Are you literally imagining kissing someone?" Pooja asked in disbelief. "Are you done? Or am I disturbing your fantasies?"

"Give me two more moments please. Yeah. OK. Done."

Pooja's mouth fell open.

"Come on, you asked me to imagine," Anant said defensively.

"OK. So, who did you imagine? Tejaswini?"

"No. Except for her, everyone else."

"What? You actually... Fine- you will say I told you to do it. But what is your conclusion?"

"That you are right. I wouldn't have minded really. As you said- no discrimination. But I wouldn't have wanted or accepted any one of them to be my girlfriend."

"See? I told you...," and then she realised what he had just said. "Did you just...?"

"Yes, I did. I said that you can consider me as your boyfriend."

She smiled, but it was in slow motion. She wasn't sure what she had heard was real, for it felt too good to be true. But as it sunk in, it made her feel very happy.

"You will remain committed, right?" she asked him after a while. "Or are you just trying me out?"

"I will remain committed," he said, and he meant it.

Krishna:

The next day, early in the morning, they heard the door to the laboratory being unlocked. The head of the department, a peon and a security guard came in. And at the very moment, Lalita walked out hurriedly without acknowledging anyone's presence. The three who came in were totally baffled to learn that there was someone behind the locked door. Krishna thought Lalita's walking out was a big mistake. He hadn't expected her to do it or he would have convinced her to wait. She should have stayed in and behaved naturally, but she was so embarrassed about thinking what they would think when they knew she was alone with a man all night, that she didn't have the nerve to face any of them. That left him alone. He was natural though, and he looked outright bored. The three men who had entered didn't say anything, but their suppressed smiles said it all. Now Krishna felt a bit embarrassed too. He thought explaining to them now how they got locked inside would sound very defensive and they would become sure that their suspicions were true. Explaining or not explaining was not going to help now that Lalita had behaved so stupidly. Well, even if she had stayed, Krishna thought, it was no guarantee that these men wouldn't have had their suspicions.

"I will take a day off today," Krishna said to the head of the department. "Had a long night last night," and he said that almost as a challenge for the men to say something.

But none spoke. They knew what kind of person Krishna was. He was always cool, but he would snap back and insult anyone and everyone if a line was crossed. They or anyone else was not going to say anything to his face- not *his* face.

Krishna was right. No one ever said anything to him. He wasn't even aware that the news had spread like wildfire throughout the staff members. It was only when Lalita found him alone once in the staff room a couple of days later that she started babbling about it.

"It's bad. They feel we locked ourselves in on purpose. They even say that we must have requested the security guard to lock us in."

"What rubbish!"

"My friend told me, and that's not all. They say it to my face. They taunt me."

"They say it to your face? I thought no one dared to say anything to you."

"Maybe I am arrogant as you think I am, but I never insult anyone as you can, and I know no one dares to speak to you on this topic, but they do it to me. Softer target, I assume, they think of me."

"And if you let them do it..."

"What do I say? How do I prove that nothing happened...?"

"You don't have to prove anything to anyone," Krishna said, quite angry now.

"That day, someone in the common room said that they are having all kinds of innovative experiments in the biology lab. I couldn't even look up to see who said that. It's becoming unbearable. You know, even if I change colleges, these rumours will follow me. The staff know one another- in all the colleges. What am I going to do? I can't afford to leave this city."

"Cool down. These things can't go on forever. They will stop."

One week later, Lalita was waiting for Krishna at his bus-stop. She knew no one else from the college staff would be there, and so she had waited. She hadn't told him that she would be waiting for him, and he was surprised to see her.

"I want to speak to you," Lalita said without waiting for Krishna to react to her presence.

"Yes, speak," said Krishna.

She opened her mouth, but no words came out. Instead, she swallowed as if trying to keep her thoughts within the confines of her body. She looked at him, and then she started biting her upper lip, then lower lip. Her eyes betrayed fear and tension.

"Lalita, speak. Calm down and speak," he said soothingly.

But she dreaded his insults, but it wasn't only that that she feared. She was afraid of what she was about to say. She kept fidgeting; she kept pushing her hair back with her fingers. But Krishna observed that there were no stray strands of hair that could possibly be tickling her face. What was disturbing her were her own thoughts.

"Lalita, I am not going to miss my bus," Krishna said, just to coax her into speaking.

At this, she looked in the direction from which she expected the bus to arrive and then she looked back at him.

"Mermee," she said, which was not more than a tiny whisper.

"What?" he asked, unable to hear her.

"Mermee," she said again a little louder, but again it was a whisper.

"Mermee? What's Mermee?"

Lalita coughed and cleared her throat.

"Marry me," she said, and blinked as if she didn't believe she had just said it clearly.

"What?" he said, shocked.

"Marry meeee," she said loudly.

"Yes. I heard you. Don't shout," he said and looked around, becoming self-conscious. "What are you talking about?" he said in what was a whisper, but still quite audible.

"I told you that day," Lalita started speaking. "These rumours will follow me wherever I go. The only thing I can do is to leave the city, but obviously I can't do that. My family is here. Family... You know my brother came to know about it. I had told my family that I had got stuck up at college that day because of some experiment, and all the phones were down. So I couldn't call. They believed me. But two days back, my brother told me that he had heard what had happened."

"How?"

"I dared not ask him. But I figured, one of his friends who is a professor at some other college, told him."

"And he believed the rumour that you and I..."

"No, he trusts me. But that is not relevant. You see that now after this, no one will marry me. You know how it works, right? A boy's family will always try to find out about the girl's character whenever a girl's family approaches with a marriage proposal. And some way or the other, they are bound to find out that I was alone with a professor from my college for an entire night."

"So, fall in love with someone, and marry him."

"Ha...," she scoffed. "What an easy alternative that you suggest. Do you think anyone will fall in love with me?"

"You are good enough."

"No. I mean after you and I were locked up for the night..."

"But why ask *me* to marry you? You can remain single."

"Krishna, do you want my parents to suffer? A daughter not getting married... You understand what..."

"But why do *you* want to suffer by getting married to me? We hate each other, remember?"

"You hate me?" she asked, surprised.

"Not now, no. But I used to."

"And I never hated you. I disliked you because you made me uncomfortable. You have impeccable logic and good knowledge of the subject. So, I knew I would not win with you in an argument, and that made me uncomfortable, and hence the dislike for you. But otherwise, I didn't have any hard feelings for you. Moreover, after that day, or rather after that night, I no longer feel the dislike too. In fact, I have..."

"You have what?"

"I have started liking you," she said and blushed a little.

"Well, I have started liking you too, but that's not love and whatever it is, it is still insufficient for us to get married."

"Do you have a girlfriend?"

"No."

"Do you love someone? I should have asked you this first, but pardon me; it didn't cross my mind as I am preoccupied with my own tensions. So, do you love anyone?"

"Not yet," he said, thinking about the chemistry professor, Supriya.

This 'not yet' reply was odd, Lalita felt, but it didn't register consciously in her mind because of what she was going through at the moment; only her subconscious mind noticed it, and so she didn't bother asking what he meant. Krishna too hadn't realised that his reply was kind of odd.

"OK," she said. "Good."

"What's good about it?"

"You are not committed to anyone; so you can marry me."

"What kind of logic is that?"

Neither of them had realised that Krishna had already missed a bus. But he had said that he would not miss a bus only to make Lalita talk. He would have willingly missed a bus or two three if it was going to help Lalita. But getting married to her...? Now, that was a bit too much.

"Only you can marry me; no one else will," she said, her face sad, but then it suddenly brightened as she said, "OK, you understand logic. So, let me put it this way."

"What way?" Krishna asked, frowning.

"Listen to me. What if my parents had approached your parents with a marriage proposal? You don't have a girlfriend. You are not in love with anyone. And my parents come to you with a proposal. What then? You would have visited us at our place. Then what would you have done? Rejected me outright?"

Krishna thought about it, looking at Lalita, trying to look at her as if she were a stranger.

"You are in fact quite good-looking; I hadn't noticed that," he said. "And you wouldn't have shown me your arrogance when I would have visited your place. So I wouldn't have known about it. You have a sweet voice as well."

Then Krishna backed away a bit to look at her, scanning her body, and her eyes widened.

"Don't do *that*," she said, embarrassed.

"You asked me to. I would have done it at your place though not that obviously."

"OK. Fine. Do that. I am standing here. Look at me," she said and looked away as Krishna's gaze continued to scan her body.

"Do you want me to turn around?" she asked, exasperated. "Or will you circumambulate around me?"

"No. No. Not necessary. I have had a good experience of your other side when you sat on the table that night and intentionally let your behind touch my hand, trying to seduce me," he said, and she totally blushed.

It took a few moments for Lalita to brush away the feeling of embarrassment.

"OK. So?" she asked, trying to suppress a smile.

"You are OK," he said.

"What? Just OK?" she said, her arrogance coming to the fore.

"Fine. It's hard to admit, but under the circumstances that you told me to imagine, I would have said yes. But what about you? What would have been your decision about me under the same arranged marriage proposal circumstances?"

"I would have said yes too."

"Hahaha... Now, you are bluffing just to convince me to marry you."

"No. Don't you get it? I wouldn't have come to you asking you to marry me if I had thought you were not good enough. I would have remained single even if it would have meant an ordeal for my parents. What do you think- I would have married anyone with whom I might have got locked up in a lab? I ask you because it's you."

"OK. I believe you. But that does not mean we are getting married."

"But why?"

"Because it doesn't make sense to get married just because we happened to get locked up in a room for a night, Lalita." (And then there is Supriya. I have no idea whether that might ever work out, but still, I can hope. But if I get married to you, that hope is lost forever.) But Krishna couldn't say any of it to Lalita.

"Krishna," Lalita said in a very serious voice, "if you hate me even now, reject me. But if you think we became friends that night, and if you think I am good enough for you, marry me because otherwise I don't think I will ever get married in this life. I know we don't love each other now, but we will. And you that day said something to me. You said you didn't know how you were ever going to make up for your insulting behaviour with me. Now's your chance. I wouldn't have said this because I know this is emotional blackmail, but my situation is desperate and if you could have married me in an arranged marriage scenario, then you can do it even now."

Krishna looked sympathetically at her, and sighed.

"OK," he said finally. "Let's get married."

"I will never be arrogant with you. You know that, right?"

"Yes, I know."

She smiled at him. Though she had not yet fallen in love with him, at this moment, she totally loved him.

After both families met and after it was official, Lalita just had to tell one random person at college about her wedding. Then the word spread and those same people who had been gossiping behind her back or taunting her, came forward to congratulate her. She could face the world again with her face up... ...and almost arrogantly.

Well, people congratulated Krishna too. But he wasn't as happy about the wedding as Lalita was and the only reason was Supriya. Krishna liked Lalita, but every time his eyes fell on Supriya, he wondered what or how it could have been, had he not been locked up with Lalita that night. Once he was going to the laboratory after his lecture when he happened to meet Supriya in the corridors.

"Congratulations," Supriya said, but without her usual cordial smile.

"Thank you," he said.

"You don't have to do it, you know," she said, her face betraying her nervousness inside her.

"Believe me," he said frankly, "I wouldn't have if there had been a choice for her."

"You don't like her, and I don't think anything happened between you two that day."

"Glad to know that you think nothing happened. Yes, nothing happened. But I do like her. I didn't initially, but after that day, I came to know of her likable side. She is not bad as I had thought her to be."

"I understand, but to get married just because she is not bad..."

"She is good," he said.

Supriya smiled.

"I know you are not lying when you say it, but still, this is a big decision," she said.

"Yes," he said. "It indeed is."

"Well then. Congratulations, again."

"Supriya," he said, calling her by her name, "I am glad that we talked. I know it doesn't mean much at this juncture, but still it means a lot to me."

She nodded and they walked away in opposite directions.

Two months before the end of the academic year, Krishna got married to Lalita. And those two months till the end of the term, it was hard for Krishna. Every time he saw Supriya, his heart ached. It was time to move on, he decided. He started giving interviews, and finally, just before the end of the term, he was selected. It was not a professor's job though. Whatever it was, he was going to accept it. It was obviously a good job, but his main intention was to leave this college to be away from Supriya as quickly as possible.

"Last day of the year, and your last day in this college too?!" Supriya said as they happened to meet in one of the corridors.

"Yes, it's better this way."

"Better for you," she said.

"Better for you too," he said.

"I hope so," she said, pain apparent in her eyes, in her voice.

"Good luck, Supriya."

"Good luck, Krishna."

They looked into each other's eyes, shook hands and smiled one last smile. They both knew they had almost never spoken to each other. They were not even friends. But they knew they had feelings for each other, and they knew that the other person was aware of it. It doesn't always require words to know the other person. It doesn't always require friendship first to fall in love. Sometimes the vibes from a person are enough to know how the person is, especially when one sees that person interacting with others day in and day out. And that's sufficient to make one like and then love that person, for love is a feeling not born out of words. Love is beyond words.

Anant:

Anant and Pooja were quite happy. There could have been nothing better than this. They met in college every day, and then they missed each other in the evenings when they went home. It was a ridiculously happy feeling for them. At times, Anant came face to face with Tejaswini, but he had never spoken to her, and though he knew she was interested in him, she didn't know he knew it, and he didn't think she could have suspected Pooja to tell him about her. So, it was never an awkward encounter. Both of them avoided looking directly at each other. Now, those who had suspected Anant and Pooja to be a couple, became quite certain that they were. The closeness between them was now quite discernible, and there no longer remained any doubt that they were indeed in love with each other. But that was what the others thought. That was mostly because of Pooja. She didn't care much to keep her love for him a secret. She would sometimes hold his hand at his elbow while walking in public; sometimes she pinched his cheek, sometimes ruffled his hair, and everything that she did when she was with him suggested her affection for him. The only way he suggested that they were a couple, was by putting up everything that she did to him with a smile on his face. Not that he didn't like it- he liked it- but he kept his hands more to himself. And the fact was that he sometimes asked himself whether he was in love with Pooja. He had never actually said to her that he loved her, but she had assumed that he did, and never pressurised him to say it. But the reason she never asked to hear it from him was because she was so happy that he was her boyfriend that she had never realised that he hadn't said it. At first, Pooja knew that he was not in love with her, but that he had only accepted to her as his girlfriend, and then time went by and she started assuming that he was in love with her- and didn't he call her all those sweet names like babe, sweetheart and darling? He too assumed at times that he had finally fallen in love with her because of her sweet nature, because he missed her when she was not around, because she was such a nice person, and because she was his closest friend. And then he did call her babe, sweetheart and darling- but was it to overcompensate or to convince himself that he loved her? Then there were times when he happened to see Tejaswini, and he used to automatically imagine what it would have been like if Pooja had not been his girlfriend. He knew that even though he himself would perhaps never have approached Tejaswini- because he thought she was out of his league,- she might have approached him some day. She had asked Pooja whether he was single, and that could only mean that she would have talked to him at some opportune time. But now he was totally committed to Pooja and these thoughts in mind were only background noise. He used to smile and brush away those thoughts, and look at Pooja as if she were all his world. A year passed and then another. They were only months away from their graduation, and by this time, Anant had almost forgotten about Tejaswini. Well, it wasn't literally forgetting her because she was still in college with him, but his mind had accepted her as a stranger to whom he *had been attracted* at some point in his life. Good that it was the past perfect tense, he thought.

It was the last day of the exams. Anant felt a lot lighter as he came out of the examination hall. He had not met Pooja for the last fortnight. Her examination centre was not the same as his, and both had decided that they would meet once their exams were over. But his and Tejaswini's centre was the same. On the first day, she had walked over to him as they were waiting outside to be let in fifteen minutes before the exam, and she had wished him luck and he had wished her the same. That was the first time they had ever talked to each other. But he had no time to dwell over it. But he had thought it was curious that people who knew each other never talked in familiar surroundings, but when they were forced into unfamiliar ones, those same people talked as if they were long lost friends.

Presently, Anant was waiting outside his centre for no particular reason. It was the final day of college for most students there. Most would not pursue higher studies, and as he realised it, he felt sad. Most of them were not going to be students anymore, but were going to live the life of an adult. He saw some familiar faces and many unfamiliar ones leaving the centre, and then he saw Tejaswini. Without giving it a thought, he approached her.

"Hi. How was it?" he asked her.

"Good. I am happy it's finally over."

"Yes. Same here," he agreed.

"So have you thought about further studies?"

"Yes. Most probably, I will be opting for post-graduation. What about you?"

"Me too, most probably, but it's not yet decided," Tejaswini said and then added, "What about Pooja?"

He became a bit self-conscious. He didn't know why, but it happened automatically.

"Yes, Pooja too," he replied.

"So you will be having company..."

"Yes," he smiled. "Have you thought about any other options if you don't opt for post-graduation?"

"No, not really. We still have time till our results. I will decide by then and then it also depends on the marks," she said.

"I don't think marks will be a problem for you."

"How do you know that?"

"You have been a bright student," he said.

"Oh, you know that?" she asked and smiled.

"Er... yes," he felt uncomfortable that she now knew that he knew she was a bright student when they had never talked.

"How do you know that?" she made him more uncomfortable.

Well, I used to look for your name on the notice boards after the results of each exam- that was how he knew, but he couldn't have said that. Wouldn't he have come to know about her being a good student from other students? Probably not, because she was not a topper, but she was always among the first five or ten students most of the time. He himself was almost always among the first five, and Pooja was between the first ten and twenty. What was he going to say? There was already a long pause now...

"So you don't know how you know that I am a bright student?"

He smiled. She had cornered him. But why? Did she know that he too had been interested in her?

"It would be embarrassing for me to tell you how I know," he said frankly.

"But why is it embarrassing? I also know you are a bright student, and I can tell you exactly how I know that. I used to look for your name after each exam result."

"You did that?" he asked, half thinking whether she had read his mind.

"Yes. Today is our last day. And we might not cross paths ever again. So I can tell you this. I was interested in you a long time back in the first year. And no one interested me after that. So you remained on my mind for the next two years too. It was nothing serious, but since I had a crush on you, I used to keep myself updated about your results. Now, you can tell me how you knew about my marks, can't you?"

"It was the same with me too. And it's embarrassing because even after Pooja and I got together, I kept looking for your name on the notice boards."

"I knew you had a crush on me," she said matter-of-factly.

"How did you know that?" he asked, surprised.

"We girls are endowed with intuition. We know such things instinctively. Even if you think you avoided looking at me, I still knew it."

"Then why didn't you..."

"Pooja was a good acquaintance. Well, not exactly a friend, but almost one. So I just wanted to know whether she had any feelings for you and I told her quite frankly that if there was nothing between you two, then.... It was a formality because I didn't feel that you were attracted to her in a romantic way. She had denied that there was anything between you two, but in a few days, I started getting a feeling that you two were really together and that made me feel so stupid that I had confided in her."

"No, she hadn't lied to you. There was nothing between us. It was only when she told me about you, after I kept pestering her to tell me about the girl who was interested in me, she realised her feelings for me."

"I was the reason? Oh! So, if I had directly approached you then... In fact, I should have done that. It was the proper way to do it. I feel so stupid now-again. But then that's fine. It was a long time back. We have grown in those two years, haven't we?" Tejaswini said with a smile.

"I don't know, but I hope so," he blurted out, not caring how it would sound.

Tejaswini's face became serious.

"Are you committed to her?" she asked.

Anant nodded. She sighed.

"We shouldn't have talked about it," she said. "To know all the facts is disturbing. It was much better not to know that I was the reason that brought you two together."

There was a pause. Neither of them knew what to say.

"I hope our paths cross again," she said, perhaps not wanting to, but she had blurted out just like Anant.

"You really want that to happen?"

"I don't know, but after talking to you it feels wrong that we may not meet again."

"I agree. But don't you think that we both are taking this a bit more seriously than we should? After all, we have never spoken to each other before. We don't know anything about each other. Maybe, you may not stand me once you start knowing me more."

"I don't deny that getting to know a person before you fall in love is not important, but some of those things are over-hyped, I think," she stated. "I personally do not believe in love at first sight, but scientifically, love at first sight exists. We as biologists know that there is nothing wrong with it. And we also know that romantic love is just a euphemism for all the raw feelings hidden deep inside our psyche. What I mean is that sometimes only vibes are enough to know a person. Think, how many times those vibes are wrong. The maximum may be fifty percent. So fifty percent of the time our guess about the other person is right. I feel my guess about your nature is right to about cent percent. That is the reason I asked whether you were committed to her. Because if you are committed- I know this about you somehow- that you will not go against your commitment."

"And I know somehow," said Anant, "about you that even if I am willing to go against my commitment, you will not let me do it."

"See? I told you vibes exist. I just hope someday sometime we meet again," she said, the disappointment of how different it could have been between the two of them, apparent in her voice.

"I want to see you again too, but I don't feel it's such a good idea," he said sadly.

"I agree, but I will still hope...," she said and looked directly and defiantly into his eyes.

Anant stared back at her. The look in her eyes softened as she perceived the pain reflected in his eyes.

"See you," Tejaswini said.

Anant nodded at her, shook her hand and she walked away. At the moment, Anant could not think about Pooja at all. He tried to bring her back into his thoughts, but all he could see was the receding figure of Tejaswini, and all he could feel was the empty feeling that came with the fact that he was probably never going to meet her again. But deep down he knew that if he and Tejaswini had not happened to talk today, it wouldn't have been that bad. He wouldn't have felt the pain that he was feeling right now. He had almost forgotten about her in the last two years- well, at least she had stopped having much effect on him, and that must have happened to her too after she had come to terms with the fact that he had a girlfriend. So now, he would just imagine no conversation ever took place between them, the way he imagined that Tejaswini would never have managed to stay with him permanently. She was out of his league, wasn't she? Or was she? He had earlier too received those vibes from her that even though she looked glamourous, she was at heart a very simple down-to-earth person. He had thought he would never talk to her, but who knew? After receiving those vibes from her, he might have eventually talked to her, if only Pooja had not been his girlfriend.

Anant could not meet Pooja that day. He couldn't have. He didn't want her to see that he had been distracted. He talked to her over the phone and feigned a headache and told her he would surely meet her tomorrow. Though she sounded disappointed, she cared for him and told him to take rest.

The next day, Anant was more into his usual groove. The disturbance in his mind had smoothed a bit, and he was now ready to meet his girlfriend. They met, and they kept meeting in their vacation before the results. Anant had once again convinced himself that he was happy with Pooja. And he was- there was no denying that. It was a fact. The 'what if' and 'if only' that had surfaced after his conversation with Tejaswini were just probabilities. Anant's reality was still Pooja.

IV

Anant and Pooja:

Soon after their results were out and they took admission for post-graduation, Anant and Pooja decided to tell their parents about their 'love'. Anant's parents liked Pooja instantly. This was Pooja's first visit to Anant's place, and he was anxious how she would react after seeing his small house. But she hadn't reacted at all. He realised that this didn't matter to her in the least. Moreover, Anant's parents liked Pooja completely. She was after all a very likable girl and person.

Some days later, Anant visited Pooja's place. He was a bit nervous as Pooja came from a much well-to-do family.

"Where do you stay?" Pooja's mother enquired.

Anant looked nervously at Pooja. But she was looking at her mother. He replied, and saw the look of disappointment flash across Pooja's mother's face as she realised that the locality belonged to the lower middle class people.

"Ah nice," Pooja's father said. "That's not that far away from here."

Anant instantly liked Pooja's father. He seemed to be the nicer of the two.

"So, you are doing post-graduation as well?" Pooja's father continued. "That's good. So what after that? Planned yet?"

"Maybe research," Anant replied.

"Very good. Very good. We have a shortage of good research scientists in our country. Hope we get one through you."

Anant smiled broadly at Pooja's father, and he smiled back. Pooja's mother's expression, however, didn't change much. She remained quite cold throughout the conversation. And when finally this 'interview' was over,

Anant felt glad to be leaving. Pooja's mother curtly waved him a bye and went inside. Pooja's father looked at his wife as if he didn't agree with his wife's behaviour. He stayed there while Pooja put her shoes on, ready to go out with Anant. Seeing Pooja busy tying her shoelaces, her father walked up to Anant.

"Don't worry," he whispered, alluding to Pooja's mother's behaviour, "she will come around. It may take some time but don't you worry. I am here to take care of that," he said pointing to the room where Pooja's mother had disappeared into.

He winked at Anant and patted on his back, and Anant smiled at this warm gesture from his girlfriend's father.

A month later, while waiting for Pooja to turn up for their date, Anant was surfing through social media sites when he happened to come across a page. There were some thousand followers following this page. But he hadn't clicked to open the page only because this high number of followers. The face in the small profile photo that he happened to see looked familiar, and when he clicked on it, he knew why. She looked different with all the makeup, but obviously, Anant could see through Tejaswini's makeup. She looked gorgeous as ever but Anant couldn't help thinking that her natural look had been much better. That layer of whatever it was on her face only veiled her beauty, Anant thought. Her profile read she was an aspiring model. No mention of her post-graduation studies! Most probably she had given up studies, and was trying to pursue a career as a model. But she was a bright student, wasn't she? Anant was thinking about the Tejaswini he knew in college, as he scrolled down her page. When he hadn't seen her in their college at the start of the academic year, he thought she had taken admission in some other college. That happened a lot after graduation. They both knew when they had talked to each other on the last day of the exam. That was the reason that they had felt they were most probably not going to see each other after that day. Most students changed colleges for post-graduation studies as not all the specialised subjects were available in all the colleges. But now, he was surprised to see that she had given up her studies. Well, he was not sure about that, but it seemed so. Or maybe, she had just taken a break. Some students did that too. They weighed their options in the real world before coming back to the academic world for further studies. As he looked at her photos, he noticed that even the career she was aiming for, would do her good. If he hadn't known who she was, he would have assumed her to be some real model- she looked that crisp, and she had obviously opted for some professional photographer who had done a great job. A thought crossed Anant's mind- had she opted out of studies because of him- because she didn't want to come face-to-face with him? What nonsense- he brushed aside the thought; he knew better than to assume himself to be the centre of anyone's life. But people made decisions depending on their past experiences, and he was surely a part of Tejaswini's life. So though not the centre, he might have been a fraction of a factor that led her to change her path. Now he thought he was indulging himself in the luxury of imagining that he had been some important part in her life or decisions. It was possible that after going home on the last day of their exams, she would have shrugged off all her thoughts about him and about the conversation they had, and become totally indifferent towards him. He enlarged some of her photos by pinching out his fingers on his phone's screen to have a good look at her face, and a feeling of yearning returned. He could have been this beautiful girl's boyfriend. Wow- she looked amazing! He scrolled down further and found a family photo. He enlarged it. Tejaswini looked so much like...

"Anant!" Anant heard a familiar voice that brought him back to his reality outside Tejaswini's page, and for a moment, he thought he had been caught looking at the photos of his first crush in college. Engrossed in his mobile phone, he had totally forgotten that he was waiting there for Pooja.

He quickly locked his phone and slipped it into his pocket.

"Hi," he said as Pooja approached him.

"Let's go," said Pooja, and as usual, held his hand at his elbow.

He looked at her as she walked with him. She was also beautiful. She was, was she not? He smiled.

Three months into the first academic year of their post-graduation, Pooja called up Anant one day after he had reached home.

"My father wants to see you," she said.

"What?" he asked surprised, and scared at what the reason might be. "Why?"

"Oh. Nothing to worry about,* she said sweetly to soothe him. "This is related to some scientific work, it seems, and he hasn't even told me yet what it is exactly about. He says he will speak to both of us at the same time."

"Oh. Fine. When?"

"Tomorrow evening after college?"

"Yes. OK."

"Great! I will tell him."

Anant told his parents that Pooja's father had called him home for a discussion on something academic, and said that he would reach home later than usual. In the evening, he and Pooja went to her place without wasting any time as they usually did by loitering around the college.

"Come in, son," Pooja's father welcomed him in. "Sit down. You too, Pooja."

They sat, and Anant looked at her father expectantly.

"I want to talk to you two about an experiment that's going on in our research wing," he began. "We have got permission from the government for human trials and we require volunteers."

"You mean human guinea pigs?" asked Pooja.

"In a way, yes," her father smiled. "And I want to know whether one of you or both would like to be just that."

"What is the experiment about?" Anant asked.

"Yes. Yes. I am coming to that. As you know, scientists all over the world are striving to enhance the human brain, to make it do feats like a computer. There have been a lot of theories and experiments about implanting chips into the brain. At our institute, we have been working on a non-invasive technique. My colleague, Prof. Wagh, has been working on this thing for the last seven years. He has devised a way to upload tons of information into the brain with nothing more than electrodes connected to the head."

Anant's eyes widened, as did Pooja's.

"It means," said Pooja, "that they may be able to upload our entire syllabus directly into our brains. And that means we will not have to study at all."

"Principally, you are right," her father agreed.

"So, if we agree to it, will they do it right away? Then they will also need to keep track of us, right?" asked Anant.

"Something like that, yes. First of all if you agree, there will be a test. Written test to see whether your brain can take such a huge data upload. If you pass that test, only then, they will give you a consent form which you will have to sign. Assuming you sign it, your brain will be uploaded with the kind of data that encyclopaedias hold. But not exactly. You may be given a choice about specific subjects, but I am nit sure of that as of now. And as Anant guessed, they will keep track of you for two years to see there are any ill effects on your brain."

"Just two years?" asked Anant.

"Well, that's the mandatory period. You will not be allowed to leave the country during this period as per the contract. After that you may choose to visit our institute periodically and tests if required will be done for free."

"But what ill effects are they referring to?" Anant enquired.

"We don't know that, to tell you frankly. Some experiments were conducted on mice, and it was observed that their problem-solving skills improved around five to seven times that of the control animals. But we can't ask mice how they feel about it; so we can't be sure. They did scan the brains of those mice to see if their pain centres were activated after the experiment, but no such thing was found. In fact, no ill effects were seen in case of the mice. The experiments also did not affect the longevity of their lives in any adverse way. Their brains were also scanned to see whether there was any damage to the cells in the long term. But none was found. But though this suggests that the experiment is safe, it has never been conducted on humans. And we don't know for sure, though I personally think that you will be alright. One more thing- if you are selected then as an incentive and because you agreed to become our 'guinea pigs', the institute will be paying an amount of money after the completion of two years which would be around four times the yearly salary of a well-paid manager in a good organisation."

Anant's eyes widened. And at that moment, he felt as if Pooja's father had told him about all this just because of the money that was involved. The difference between the standard of living of Pooja's family and his family was a large one, and Anant had always been conscious about it. Pooja's mother, he knew, was in one of the rooms of this apartment at this moment, but she hadn't even come to greet him. If Anant was selected in this experiment, the money will give him some base to start his life. He may invest, he may...

"Don't count your chickens yet though," Pooja's father said as if he had read Anant's mind. "We require two volunteers, and we may get a lot of prospective candidates. Toppers will be selected. First two. But there is one more condition. If those toppers fall short of the required parameters, they will not be selected. Then there will be another round of tests."

"What are these tests? IQ tests?" asked Pooja.

"Hmmm... Not exactly. It is a combination of IQ test, aptitude, your skill at problem-solving and they will also be testing your Emotional Quotient, your predisposition to commit crime..."

"What?" Pooja asked, surprised.

"Your brain will be stuffed with so much knowledge. What if you use that to become a criminal who can commit perfect crimes?" said her father.

Anant was glad that this information was shared with him. He didn't know whether he could pass the exam, but he would look out for the questions that might project him as an aggressive person. He was aggressive; he now remembered how he had tackled the students who were ragging the juniors. Anant decided he would keep his eyes open for those specific questions and try to project himself as a very peace-loving or even a timid individual.

"When are they conducting the first test?" he asked Pooja's father.

"This Sunday is the test, and assuming all goes well, before the start of the next month, your brains will be encyclopaedias."

"What?" said Pooja.

"There isn't any acclimatisation period. If selected, your brain will just be uploaded with the data. So basically, if you don't count the follow-ups, you will be required to visit our institution only twice or thrice, once for the test, one more time for the data upload and I am keeping a third as a buffer- I think the selected candidates may want to discuss something more with us."

"Whose consent is required?"

"Candidates who are only above eighteen can volunteer, and so only their consent is enough."

"This is quite interesting," Anant said. "Didn't you think of doing it on yourself?"

"I am not a very young man. Prof. Wagh in fact did ask me whether I was interested, but I thought maybe the younger generation should give it a try. Wagh cannot do it on himself though. He is the main inventor of this procedure and though we say it is quite safe, we still do not want to risk anything happening to Wagh. What if something were to go wrong- then we would want the man behind the experiment to make that wrong right."

Anant was in two minds about disclosing this to his parents. They deserved to know. What if something went wrong after the experiment- they wouldn't even know what happened to him, and who to approach. Obviously, Pooja's father would assist, but still they deserved to know. But again, he wasn't so sure about it. If he let them know that this was an experiment involving his brain, then suddenly Pooja and her family would turn into villains for them. Anant kept this decision pending for later. He would take the written test first. If he didn't get selected, there was no use telling his parents.

The Test:

Pooja was waiting at the entrance of the institute for Anant. They went up to the fifth floor together. The waiting area was full. But there weren't more than forty candidates. It was surprising, Anant thought, that the incentives hadn't attracted a lot of people. Maybe because the brain was involved, it has scared most people away. Or maybe because it was a huge sum of money, people had suspected something to go wrong. But the incentives were most probably so that people would stay in the country for regular follow-ups. They would receive them only after two years.

The test was online on a computer. Though Pooja's father had mentioned a written test, it wasn't literally a written test. Anant noticed that once an answer was submitted, he couldn't go back to the question. His time was being clocked. He hurried now. He wanted to be in the top two. He had always been in the top five for the last three years in college, and there were always more than forty students in his class. So he had a chance. But this was different. He knew this thing was more competitive than those college exams. Most students didn't study that well. In fact, if he had wanted to he could have been in the top three or even the topper, but he hadn't cared for that. But here... this wasn't based on a syllabus. This made it more competitive. FInally, he submitted his last answer, but didn't realise it. He waited expecting the next question, but instead a man approached his desk and quietly asked Anant to follow him. When he got up, he was surprised to see that all the other candidates were still anchored to their chairs. Had he been too fast? Did he make some mistakes? Was he being taken out because he was discarded as being a dull candidate?

"Go to that room there," the man who had bright Anant out told him. "You will be required to give an interview."

"An interview?"

"Yes. As you must have noticed, you were the first one to complete the test, and you passed. Obviously, there is still a possibility that someone may get a higher score, but your score surpassed the minimum requirement."

"Oh! Thank you," Anant said to the man and started walking towards the room he had pointed to.

Suddenly, he realised that the test he had just attempted didn't have any questions that would be able to judge his predisposition to crime. Oh, so the interview was for... Pooja's father hadn't mentioned any interview. Perhaps he wasn't allowed to say anything about it. But he had told them about the 'crime' predisposition thing all the same.

"Have a seat," one of the three interviewers said to Anant.

Anant deliberately sat down clumsily, dropping his bag on purpose, feigning pressure. He felt the pressure, but some of it was feigned.

"What would you do if someone tried to rob by pointing a knife at you and you had a pistol at your disposal?"

Anant was genuinely startled at this question. There was no introduction- nothing. The interview had started abruptly.

"A pistol with me? But why would a person with a knife try to rob a person who has a pistol?" he said.

"The robber doesn't know that you have a weapon. He asks you to empty your pockets and as you do, you have the opportunity to take the pistol out."

"Well, it seems logical that I will point the pistol at him and tell him to leave," Anant said, and though he knew this answer might seem aggressive, it was only logical that he shouldn't get robbed when that can be prevented.

"What if the robber remains unfazed and thinks it's a bluff- that you wouldn't use the pistol on him?"

Ah, thought Anant, now that was the real question.

"Well then, he would be right in assuming so. I wouldn't use the pistol on him even if it means I have to give my money to him. If he remains unfazed, he might be in need of the money."

"So, you will not defend yourself when you can? Even the law allows it in self-defence."

"I cannot kill a man even if the law allows it."

"Another scenario- your friend's life is at stake. If you don't use your gun, your friend dies."

"I will request. If that doesn't work, it leaves me no choice. Better a robber dead than my friend," Anant said and thought these questions weren't challenging enough.

"But you can miss your aim and hit your friend instead."

"If I don't use the gun then, as you said, my friend dies for sure. If I use the gun, there is a fifty percent chance that he survives."

The interviewer smiled.

"But will you be able to live with the guilt that you killed your own friend?"

"Better to live with the guilt that I killed him trying to save him, rather than live with the fact that I didn't do anything to save him."

"But you will have blood on your hands. If you don't use the gun, the blame would be on the other man."

"No, the blame would still be on me," Anant said, but he realised that he was failing the interview- he was not projecting himself as someone who would be passive or timid or peaceful in the face of a life and death situation; he was just using logic, but so be it; his logic was always strong- he could not remain passive if he could change the situation.

"What if he is that friend who had once tried to woo your girlfriend away from you?"

"If he had done that and he is still my friend, then there must be something in him that has kept the friendship alive. I will still try to save him."

"Let us say, he snatched your girlfriend away from you and now if he dies, you get your girlfriend back."

"If he managed to get my girlfriend, then my girlfriend is equally to blame at least from my perspective. I wouldn't want my girlfriend back. But if you allow me to indulge in logic, I would like to add that if I use the gun and kill the robber, my friend now owes me something in future. Even if I happen to kill my friend, then in a way, I got my revenge. I wouldn't want that- just because he wooed away my girlfriend does not mean he should die for it- but then logically, if I use the gun, I win whatever the result. As it is my friend was going to die, better at the hands of someone he did wrong to once."

The interviewers looked at one another.

"You wait outside," one of them said; the interview was over as abruptly as it had started.

Anant was confused. This was an odd interview. There was only one right answer to those questions. Even a timid person would do the same things in such scenarios as he had suggested. He looked around. He saw no candidates leaving the test room. After around fifteen minutes, Anant was called in again. He was surprised to see Pooja's father there.

"I came in from the other door," he said to Anant, reading his mind. "You are selected."

Anant looked at him wide-eyed.

"What happened to the other candidates?" he asked.

"They all failed the written test. *All* of them, and they have already left the facility from the other door in that room," Pooja's father said, stressing on the word 'all' to indicate that even Pooja had failed.

"But you required two candidates."

"None of them crossed the threshold requirements. And since we have you, we decided to go with just one instead of the originally intended two."

"I just have a doubt," Anant said tentatively.

"Ask."

"Those questions that you asked me here seemed to have clear-cut answers at least when thought logically..."

"Yes, the interview was to test your logic, and your integrity. Moreover, it wasn't just yes or no. You explained yourself logically- why you would do a certain thing- that impressed us."

"Oh. I am glad I could do that."

That evening, Anant went to Pooja's place.

"But you had said they would be testing me for my crime predisposition," Anant said to Pooja's father as soon as he settled down.

"Your answers made the interviewers change their questions. They did that after the third or the fourth question- they hadn't expected the explanations and they got a bit stumped. They could still have brought the interview back on course after they asked you your last question. But the explanation that you gave for your last answer- that changed it all. They couldn't have been more impressed. The interview went haywire as far as they were concerned. They changed the purpose of the interview from the 'crime predisposition of the subject' to 'logical integrity analysis of the subject'," Pooja's father checkled.

"They can do that?"

"Who would object when one of the interviewers was Prof. Wagh himself?"

"I didn't know he was there."

"The one sitting at the centre of the table was him."

"You two," said Pooja, "are talking to each other as if I am not here at all. And you, Anant, you didn't even say 'hi' to me. You just came and started talking to my father, and he too started responding as if you two know each other from before I introduced you two."

Anant smiled at her.

"Sorry, Pooja," he said apologetically. "I had questions on my mind since the time I left the institute, and I was getting impatient."

"And no one even cares that I wasn't selected," she said pouting.

"No one except Anant was selected," Pooja's father said to her. "That means there is nothing wrong with you. However, it seems that there is something wrong with your boyfriend."

"No. Nothing's wrong with him," she said defensively. "He is just good at what he does."

"And this wasn't an IQ test really," her father said. "It was a mixture of tests. You really don't have to feel bad about not getting selected. It wasn't a failure of any kind."

But then her father looked at Anant, and Anant had a feeling that the test had much more to do with IQ than Pooja's father was suggesting."

"What happens next?" Pooja asked, taking the topic back to Anant's selection in the experiment.

"Oh yes," said Pooja's father more to Anant than to his daughter, "I asked Wagh whether you can get any choice in the data that is uploaded into your brain. Basically, it doesn't matter because you are going to be one of the most knowledgeable persons on earth. But if you have a preference, you can tell me and I will ask Wagh whether it can be done."

"I have a preference. My main subject in junior college was biology. So even now, it's the same. I would have opted for physics if I had been good at mathematics. I liked physics, but numbers make me dizzy."

Pooja giggled as she too shared some of her boyfriend's dizziness with numbers.

"Yes," said Anant, smmiling, "they do make me dizzy. So if they could upload all the theories in physics with the related maths, I would love it. I would love to become a physicist without having to study maths. So if it is all going to be automatically stored in my brain without me having to sweat for it, then nothing like that. That is my first preference, then chemistry and then perhaps biology if there is more space available in my brain," he smiled.

"Why don't you opt for biology?" Pooja asked. "That way, you will not need to study at all, and I too will get all the help I require from you."

"He is not opting for biology because he is not lazy," Pooja's father said to Pooja. "He wants the subjects he won't normally study or have access to, to be uploaded to his brain, and he can take care of biology by the normal way of studying. Is that correct, Anant?"

Anant nodded.

"But I think," continued Pooja's father, " that quite a part of your academic syllabus will also be uploaded because they will upload all information they think is important. They will upload your brain with the constitution, the law and some other subjects even if you don't want them. First they will make you a jack, and then they will try and make you a master of the trade that you prefer."

Pooja shook her head, disagreeing at the way in which her father had used the proverb, but she was smiling all the same time.

This time too, Anant noticed, Pooja's mother wasn't there to congratulate him.

"Is your mother there?" Anant asked Pooja.

"Yes," Pooja said, but she looked uncomfortable.

"Can you call her here?" he asked.

Pooja looked at her father who looked a bit surprised, but he nodded at his daughter, suggesting that she call her mother out. She went in and within a minute, she and her mother returned to the hall. Anant got up from his chair and went and touched Pooja's mother's feet; she was so shocked at this gesture that she froze.

"Need your blessings, madam," he said. "I am a bit nervous..."

Pooja's mother awkwardly placed her hand on Anant's head and then grabbed his arm and pulled him up.

"Do well," she said. "And congratulations on your selection."

"Thank you," he said and grinned at her; she had to smile back. "I will take your leave," he said to Pooja's parents. "Thank you for this opportunity."

Pooja's mother stood there feeling uncomfortable for a few moments and then went back to her room as Pooja started wearing her socks and putting on her shoes, ready to leave with Anant.

"What was that about? And don't you need my blessings?" Pooja's father asked Anant in a whisper.

"I know your blessings are always with me," Anant said, but bent down to touch his feet, but he didn't let him. He instead patted Anant's back like he had done the last time too.

"I suspect what you did with her was only to make her feel embarrassed and make her feel guilty," Pooja's father said.

Anant bit his tongue to convey that Pooja's father's guess was correct and that he was sorry for doing that, but his eyes twinkled with mischief.

"What are you two smiling at?" asked Pooja.

"It's between him and me," Pooja's father said and smiled at his daughter.

"I have started feeling that *he* is your son," said Pooja to her father.

ꕤ

The Experiment:

As Anant left Pooja's place, he realised he had still to make the decision of whether he was going to tell his parents what he was going to do. Though he wanted to be selected, he hadn't expected that he would actually pass the test. He now wanted to share his success with parents as well and wanted to tell them about the experiment, but he wasn't really sure that it would be a very good idea. Right now, Pooja was with him, and so he pushed the pending decision away from his mind. He would think about it when he was alone.

That day when Pooja left, and Anant was walking back home alone, he knew he had to think about what to tell his parents. But as he thought about it, he started predicting his parents' reactions.

Have you lost your mind completely? How can you trust someone you just met?

Pooja seems to be a fine girl, but I wouldn't trust her parents.

Your brain, Anant, your brain is at stake! What if you become paralysed for the rest of your life or go mad?

I think they don't want their daughter going out with you, but instead of trying to convince Pooja- she may rebel against them- they are trying to manipulate and play with the only thing you have got- your brain; once you lose control over your own mind, even Pooja will not stay with you. That's their plan- don't you get it?

I thought something was fishy about this man when you told us that he readily accepted your friendship with Pooja. Which girl's father would want his only daughter to be married off to someone poor? Now, we see the conspiracy.

Hadn't we told you to stay away from rich girls? Now you start trusting Pooja's parents more than your parents.

Anant shuddered as the thoughts came rushing in. Were those thoughts really what his parents would think? Or were they what he himself was thinking? Did he not trust Pooja's father? Did he want Anant to lose his mind so that his daughter could marry a better boy? But Anant trusted Pooja's father. But was that because Anant was gullible or was her father really trustworthy? Now, Anant was the one who had started suspecting conspiracy.

Don't you see? Only you were selected. Why? Do you think you are that intelligent that no one but you could pass the test?

But hadn't he completed the test first?

You completed the test first, but that does not mean you answered all the questions correctly. And why would they not call anyone else for the interview? Because they didn't want any of the other candidates.

Now, who would really go to such an extent as to call some forty candidates and reject them?

What had they got to lose? They weren't paying any of the candidates to appear for the test. And what an opportune time! You visit Pooja's place and in a couple of months, they are ready with an experiment. Is that coincidence?

Anant was imagining a lot. He decided not to tell his parents. He was shaken by his own thoughts. He would go ahead and sign the contract.

Correct- that contract- it will free them of all responsibility. We won't even be able to file a case against them for our only son. If something happens to you, only we will suffer. No one's going to come and look after you.

But they had government approval for human testing. Anant was going to go ahead- he wasn't going to miss out on this once in a lifetime opportunity.

The day came. Nervously, Anant went to the institute. It was a Sunday and his parents thought he was going on a small trip with Pooja for the entire day. His hand was trembling when he signed the contract. Pooja was waiting in a room along with her father while Anant's head was connected with the electrodes. His wish had been granted. Physics and mathematics were going to be uploaded in his brain with some chemistry too. Some technology, law, constitution and an entire encyclopaedia, all for free, and then after two years, he would also receive the incentive. He had checked the contract for that especially, and nominated his parents in case anything were to happen to him within those two years. But his parents did not know, and if anything happened to him today, they might never know. But Pooja- he trusted her. At least, she would see to it that his parents got the money they deserved.

Anant lay on his back, and then he heard a switch flip on. Then some flashes danced in front of his eyes- so fast that he could not decipher a single thing. Was he... did he... had he taken the right decision? His brain could not cope up with the tornado of information being uploaded into it. He passed out, but the machine did not stop. It stopped only when it was done with him. The upload was complete.

Anant opened his eyes. And then he instantly closed them. He felt dizzy. He could stand the light in the room. After a couple of minutes, he opened his eyes again.

"What time is it?" he remembered that he was at the institute; so far so good; he was sane at least at the moment.

"It's 12 o'clock," Pooja replied standing at his bedside. "Don't worry about the time. How are you feeling?"

It was around two and half hours since he had blacked out.

"I am feeling dizzy, but otherwise fine. Is that because of the mathematics that they uploaded," he joked weakly and Pooja and her father laughed.

"Feeling dizzing is fine," Pooja's father said reassuringly.

"But I am not feeling any different. It feels like the same old me," Anant said, sounding a bit disappointed.

"What is 446 into 869?" Pooja's father asked him.

"387574," said Anant lazily. "Why?"

And then he opened his eyes wide. How did he know that?

"How do I know that? Was that even correct?" he asked.

Pooja's father opened the calculator application on his mobile.

"Yes," he confirmed. "You are correct."

Pooja almost hugged Anant, but realising her father was also there, she backed away, but kept grinning at him. She felt so proud of him.

"You asked for mathematics," Pooja's father said. "And they uploaded some basic tables too."

"But I can use a calculator for that. They could have uploaded some more useful information."

"They have done that too. What is the mass of a neutrino?"

"0.07"

"0.07 what?" asked Pooja's father.

"0.07 eV," replied Anant.

"You see what happened just now? You didn't bother to mention the unit of the mass. That means you assumed that it was obvious to others that you were not referring to the mass in terms of kilograms or grams. The information is so ingrained in your brain that you feel like it has been there for years."

Pooja grinned again.

"Go on, hug him if you want to. Don't worry about me. I am not looking."

Pooja came and awkwardly hugged Anant, who smiled an embarrassed smile.

Prof. Wagh was intimated that Anant was conscious now. After about two hours of basic tests on him- some medical tests and some pertaining to the experiment, he was 'discharged' from the institute. Pooja, her father and Anant went home together. Anant had a small meal at their place. Pooja's mother came out of her room to see Anant. She did it without being coaxed to do so. She was curious to know what had happened to him- how he had changed. Anant flaunted some of his knowledge. She looked impressed. She knew if all went well, Anant would no longer be remaining poor, and she wasn't thinking about the incentive money, but about the priceless information in his brain. For the first time, it seemed as if she was fine with her daughter being with Anant. Pooja's father felt proud. He knew it was because of him that Anant was now what he was. He couldn't stop asking Anant intermittently some random multiplications and divisions. And every time, Anant answered, he looked at his wife as if to say 'See- I always told you he was a bright boy.' Anant now had no suspicions at all about all this being a conspiracy. Pooja's mother couldn't stop herself from asking Anant a few questions of her own, and she found it amusing that he knew their answers.

"How does it feel?" she asked and Anant beamed at her, for this was not some random question out to test his knowledge, but a personal question.

"It feels odd," said Anant. "I mean in an exam, for example, I read a question, and then to answer it, I think about it. When my brain finds the answer to that question, it visualises the text that I have read. My brain knows where I have read it. Even if it does not always remember where I have read the answer, it still knows that I have read it somewhere- that it is acquired through some efforts on my part. But now when you ask me something and if the answer comes out of the database that was uploaded into my brain, it feels like an automatic answer. It is a sort of reflex. It seems like it was always there. We don't tell a baby that if it is hungry he should put food in his mouth. It comes naturally. A baby cannot put food in his ear when it is hungry. It's always the mouth. It is an instinct. The answers that come out of the database feel like instinct because I don't remember having read about them or even acquired them. They seem like some sort of genetic memory. My brain doesn't even consciously know that it knows the answer, but it's there. It's weird, but it feels extremely good to have whatever this is. It feels like power."

"There could have been no better description," said Pooja's father.

Pooja was quite silent as she looked at the three of her favourite persons talking to one another. It felt wonderful, especially to see her mother and Anant talking to each other. But Anant kept looking at his girlfriend from time to time. He wanted her to be a part of this conversation too. He was content to see that she felt happy about all this.

"Should I drop you home?" Pooja's father asked as Anant stood up to leave.

"No, it's fine. I feel normal."

"I will be with him," Pooja said.

"Call me up if you don't feel good, even in the slightest."

"Yes, I will," said Anant.

"And don't forget the follow-up dates. I will also be reminding you."

"Yes. Sure. I think they uploaded those dates too in my brain," Anant joked and they all laughed.

Though he felt all normal in his wakefulness, Anant's sleep that night was extremely disturbed as his brain coped up with the information that it was fed with that day, and this trend of disturbed sleep continued for a week more. But gradually, his brain adjusted to its power, and let Anant sleep soundly once again. Pooja's father had been right. Though Anant's brain had not been explicitly uploaded with the current syllabus, there was so much information in his brain that he didn't have to work much for his exams. But the practicals were a different thing altogether. Though he had the information, he didn't have the dexterity to put that knowledge into practice, and he had to work as hard in the laboratory as he had needed to before this experiment was performed on him. For the time being, he had abstained from showing his super powers to any one in college. But the powers weren't going to remain hidden for long, for he sometimes seemed to know more than the professors. He sometimes couldn't stop himself from asking questions that no one understood or from answering other students' questions, which the professors could not. But even then, no one was going to know what had happened to him. The secret was safe with him and Pooja. Anant had still not told his parents, but they too were sometimes surprised at some things he said all of a sudden or of the solutions he seemed to have for most problems. Sometimes he would just look at the symptoms of someone sick and guide them to the proper doctors.

"How?" his father asked him once.

"I am studying biology. I know about diseases and conditions," Anant replied, but he knew that this was out of his syllabus.

Sometimes, Anant's thoughts took him out on a tour. This wasn't something new, and it happened to everyone, he knew. But when one had so much information in his brain, sometimes there was no stopping the thoughts that kept coming non-stop one after the other. This happened especially when he thought about science. The laws, the theories, the hypotheses all led to one thing- his own speculations. And then he would get lost totally in his own world.

"Anant? Anant? ANANT!" it was Pooja, calling him.

They were sitting in the library, and he had gone off in his own world. He was reading a book, and then something that he read there had started a chain of thoughts, and then he had become so totally engrossed in his world that when Pooja said that they have had enough of the studies for today and that they should leave now, he didn't respond. Pooja looked at him to check whether he had fallen asleep, but he hadn't. And then she thought something was wrong with him.

"We should go to the institute," she insisted.

"No. Believe me, I was thinking about a theory. I hadn't passed out with my eyes open. If you want to hear what I was thinking, I will tell you."

"No. No, it's fine. I believe you," Pooja said quickly, because nowadays most of what he said pertaining to science, went quite a few feet over her head.

It had now been three months since the experiment. Anant had visited the institute five times in this period. Just the usual follow-ups. Nothing seemed wrong with him. Prof. Wagh had looked quite satisfied all those five times. Anant felt normal too- as normal as he could feel with all that knowledge in brain and with the ensuing chain of thoughts.

Then came a day when a thought came coming back again and again. It wasn't a glitch in Anant's brain. It was just that he had got hooked on a problem- a question that he himself had created. It was a problem in physics. Physicists had theorised a particle for light. It was called a photon. They had a particle for gravity- the graviton. There were particles that described how forces worked. Physics, in fact, had a particle ready for all things that intuitively looked like waves. But there wasn't a particle for time. Could time be explained on the basis of a particle? As one thought led to another and then another, Anant started feeling that time could be explained on the basis of its own particle, and a parallel thought also kept surfacing in his mind, and it was that time did not exist. Perhaps Time was only a function of matter. Time existed only because there was matter or mass in the universe. Remove all the matter from the universe, and time and space may not exist at all. Mass was something that created the universe, it seemed to Anant. But then what was mass? Mass was basically precipitated energy. So then what was time? It was a by-product of mass. And yet time could be explained in terms of a particle as well.

Anant wrote down his thoughts as they came. In about fifteen days, his hypothesis on time was ready. As he revisited his writings, a new possibility seemed possible. Two days later, he went to a market and brought home an odd rubbery fabric and a few lithium-ion batteries. In the days that followed, he brought home small things that sometimes looked odd and sometimes mundane if seen through the eyes of layman- USB connectors, four digital watches, a wireless keyboard- one which could be connected to mobile phones, soldering iron and a few such things. He folded the fabric, took measurements, cut it and stitched it. He kept doing odd things in the dead of the night, and he did that with nothing more than a pencil and a few pieces of paper to note down his thoughts or calculations. There were no books required. He had all the books in his brain. He told no one what he was doing, not even Pooja. His parents knew he was on to something. But they did not bother him much, assuming that he was working on some project for his college.

"What is it for?"

"It's a prototype, not much functional," Anant lied.

"OK. Whatever. We won't understand much about it even if you try to explain."

But even if Anant's parents couldn't have understood how it worked, they would have guessed what it did, had he simply told them that it was a space-time-machine.

The Space-Time-machine:

The space-time-machine was ready now. Anant had to test it. Along with the main machine that could carry him, he had also built a miniature one. But this miniature one was built with another functionality as well. It was to destroy itself once it made the time leap. He adjusted the dials so that this miniature machine leapt two minutes into the future, stayed there for five seconds, then came back to the time from which it was sent and destroyed itself. Rechecking the time on the dials, Anant hit a button. The small machine vanished in front of his eyes and then it reappeared at the same moment as if it had not vanished at all, and then it exploded leaving just flames in its place.

"What was that noise?" asked his mother.

"Nothing," I dropped something," Anant said, blowing off the fumes towards the window. He had built in the self-destruct feature because if the machine hadn't worked as intended, he didn't want it to fall into wrong hands. He was totally elated that it had worked. The time-machine was supposed to go two minutes into the future to a place which was not far away from where he was right now. He had programmed it to be just two metres away from where it had been. Whether it had actually been there, he was soon going to find out. But it seemed it had worked perfectly. It had come back to its time of origin. That's why the moment it disappeared, it had conjured back at the same spot, and then destroyed itself. He waited with baited breath now. Thirty seconds to go now. Twenty. Ten. Anant now focussed his eyes on the spot two metres away from him at which the space-time-machine should appear from two minutes into the past. He stood up and walked towards the spot. And then it appeared out of nowhere. He stared at it. He did nothing, but to stare at it for five seconds and then poof... It vanished. Anant knew it had gone to the same time from which it was sent here and destroyed itself. The smell from its destruction still lingered in the room. Anant had built a machine that could not only time-travel, but could also teleport in space. He now turned back and looked at the main larger life-sized machine; he stared at it. He had invented something that no man or woman had ever invented. Every physicist's dream had just come true for him. Anant smiled- it was the smile of a mad man, for what he had built, he could share with no one. And his wild expression was just an outlet for the inexplicable feeling that churned and wriggled inside him.

To achieve something and not being able to share it with anyone is troublesome. Anant had built a time-machine, but he could not share his achievement with anyone. It was a dangerous machine. If such a thing ever fell in the hands of a wrong person, it could have devastating effects. He trusted his parents, he trusted Pooja, he trusted Pooja's parents- at least her father- too, but he still didn't want to share his secret with anyone. He decided he would think about it and might confide about the machine with one or all of them. But presently, he thought, it would be best if no other soul knew about it. He hadn't yet thought about the repercussions of having and using such a thing. He had tested the miniature machine. And he was confident that the larger one would work as intended. But he had tested the smaller one in the confines of his home. He was the only one who had seen it as it travelled to the future and back. He was the only one who had seen it intact when in fact it had already been destroyed two minutes earlier. It was like seeing a ghost. It was like meeting a person after he was cremated. But the machine that he had seen two after it was destroyed was not a ghost. It was a real thing. Anant knew the meaning of this. Time-travel created paradoxes. Cause and effect may no longer maintain their natural order. An effect could come before cause. An effect could become a cause of its own cause. It could be confusing. He would have to tread this path cautiously and very carefully, Anant knew. Yet, he was eager to test his machine- to be inside it and go to some other time. Moreover, it was not just a time-machine, it was a space-time-machine. And to teleport in space was no less a feat than to time-travel. He had achieved both in a single machine. Thanks to Pooja's father and Prof. Wagh, Anant had just become brilliant.

Anant was restless- completely impatient. But he still hadn't used the machine. He would do it this weekend. On Saturday, he met Pooja at her place after college. He was going to take her out for an early dinner. In fact, he met her at her place because he wanted to see her father. He wanted to meet him for no real reason. Anant was just getting emotional since he had decided that he would be using the machine tonight. Then he took Pooja out. It was still quite early, and he didn't eat much because he also wanted to have something that could be called a dinner with his parents. After his date, he and Pooja walked to her place hand-in-hand. When they were in the lift of her building, he pulled her close and kissed her sensuously. She just hoped that the lift doors would not open. But they did.

"What's up with you today?" she asked as the doors opened. "It was damn good."

"I know," he smiled.

"Coming in?" she asked.

"No. Some other time. As it is, I met your father just this evening. It may seem odd."

"Yes. OK."

He looked at her one final time, and then let the doors of the lift close. At home, he again had some food with his parents.

"You are hungry? Didn't you have anything with Pooja?" his mother asked.

"Saved some space for the home-cooked food."

"That's better. Home-cooked food is always healthy," said Anant's father.

Anant lingered a bit till their dinner was over. Then he quietly went and freshened up. He set his hair with his hands in front of the mirror- the machine would be taking him out. He opened a small bag of cloth in which he had folded up the space-time-machine, which was made from the rubbery fabric. After the lights switched off, he put the bag in his pocket and then got inside the machine. He was nervous, tense. He didn't know whether he would see this same world around him when he came back- *if* he came back. Though he knew time-travel could create paradoxes, he was ready to test them. In all the information that had been uploaded in his brain, there were many speculations on what could happen in case of time-travel. But every argument had a counter-argument, and all the arguments seemed to be logically correct. Anant had his own theory of what would happen; he tended to incline towards some arguments more than others. But right now, it was not his intention to test any of these arguments; he did not intend to create any paradoxes. He just wanted to time-travel to have an experience and to test his machine. Later on maybe, he would test different theories and their logic, but at this moment, he wanted to stay away from all of it. He would go and come back and nothing would change- he tried to convince himself. He breathed in deeply and clicked on a button on the digital watch which was a part of the machine. The light of the display switched on. He held his breath. Where was he going to go? He had decided that already, for he remembered that day of his life vividly. He remembered the date and the time of that day quite precisely. He would reach there a bit early and try to nullify it. Though he remembered the day clearly because of that particular episode, nullifying that episode wouldn't have any effect on his life. In fact, it would save a lot of trouble for others, he had supposed so.

The Time-Travel:

Presently Anant breathed out and the faces of his dear ones flashed before his eyes- his mother, father, Pooja and Pooja's father too. He again took a deep breath and then as he pressed on a button, suddenly Tejaswini's face flashed before his eyes. As the time-machine swung into action, he felt faint, and everything seemed to spin around him, and the next moment, it stopped. Basically, not even a moment had passed- it had happened in that same single moment but he still had this weird feeling in his stomach that one has in a free-fall. Then the feeling stopped abruptly. Everything that he had felt had just lasted a single moment, less than a fraction of a second, and he was grateful for that. He remembered that just a few seconds earlier as his mind had thought about his dear ones, it had not missed out on Tejaswini. He still liked her, didn't he? Sometimes a stray thought made him think how she was. Sometimes he visited her page, but only saw some more glamourous photos- nothing personal. But to think of her before his first time-travel mission meant that she was much more important to him than he consciously thought she was. He sighed and looked around. It was daytime, but these stairs where he had appeared were the ones at the backside, and as he had expected, they were deserted. He quickly started getting out of his machine, but then he stopped. He might need it in an emergency. The machine looked odd on him, but not odder than a boiler suit. Anant pushed down the hood that covered his head and started walking towards the voices he heard. He stood at the point where the stairs reached the ground floor. He turned round the corner and watched. It was quite dark where he was standing, and that in conjunction with the fact that his boiler suit was dark-coloured, he knew he wouldn't be visible. He was now in two minds. The original plan he had thought of had been simple, that of confrontation. But now that he had time-travelled, he realised that he had made the plan without taking into account that his machine would be with him. With the machine, confrontation seemed risky. What if he lost his machine or something happened to it. Well, actually, he had built that machine with nothing special and he could rebuild it, but he didn't want to get stuck in a timeline in which he did not belong, for more than was necessary. He was in the college- his college- but the day was not today- it was the day when he had first set his foot here. It was a day when a senior had stopped him and ushered him to a corridor which was empty except for a few seniors and a group of frightened juniors. He was now standing at the other end of the corridor. He was early here today. The Anant from the past would not be here for around fifteen minutes more. Anant could see all the seniors there. The large boy who had blocked his way was also there. He would later go and block the younger Anant, unless the older Anant... The seniors were ragging a small boy. The same old scene, it was, that Anant had seen. They were trying to make him undress and dance, shaking his buttocks, but he was not doing it because a girl was also there among the seniors. Sheela- Anant remembered. It would be humiliating to undress and shake a buttock in front of a girl who was just two years older to him. Anant had come here so that the younger Anant would not need to confront the seniors. He had got them suspended. He had liked that, but what was the use of all that? Today, he could have confronted them as their senior (those same students who were two years senior to him at the time he had joined this college were now a year younger than him), and threatened them with a complaint, but now the machine that he had with him seemed to make him think twice about a direct confrontation. But then as he thought about the machine, a wild idea formed in his mind. What if... Anant checked the dial that showed the power in the batteries of his machine. All the batteries were full. He could use the space-time-machine to teach these seniors a lesson without getting them suspended and without making the younger Anant go through the trouble of physically restraining his seniors. The younger Anant could directly go to his class and sit beside Pooja for the entire lecture. He looked at the seniors, marked their positions in his mind's eye. He then programmed his machine. This larger machine was also programmable like its smaller version to auto-time-travel. Anant had built this larger version before the smaller one. But when he had made the smaller version programmable to auto-time-travel for testing purposes, he had also added this feature in the larger machine. It was now coming in handy.

Anant finished the programming. It was going to start in 30 seconds. He saw the leader of the ragging group brandishing scissors in front of the boy. Ten seconds more. The boy looked all the more frightened. And then the senior lost his scissors. It happened so fast that he didn't even realise it. Anant had just teleported to the spot where the senior was standing, snatched his weapon and teleported back to the stairs- in a split-second. The senior was brandishing his hand in front of the junior as if he were still holding the scissors. Anant's work had not been finished yet. Now, round two began and ended a minute into the future, and this future was coming to meet them as each second passed. But as of now, the ragging group was still laughing at the junior. Anant had done his part and was now waiting to see the result. The senior threatened once again and brought down his empty hand towards a loop of the junior student's pants. And then he realised- his hand was empty. He looked around, searched his pockets, asked his friends including Sheela if they had seen his scissors, but no one had. And at that moment, it happened. It was odd. It was as if they all had hallucinated at the same time- because what happened couldn't have been real. Most of the juniors saw it. It was like a wave that appeared around the group of the seniors, stayed for a split-second, and then disappeared. But after a few seconds, chunks of hair started falling off from the heads of the ragging group. The juniors stared as the perfect-looking heads of the seniors moments before now looked like fields trampled by a herd of elephants. The ragging group looked at one another as a few hair still continued to fall off their heads. The juniors too looked at one another to check whether whatever that had happened to their seniors had happened to them as well. But they were relieved to find that they were alright. Sheela shrieked. She touched her head in alarm. But she, like the juniors, didn't seem to have been affected. The leader along with his friends looked totally stumped. Bald spots on their heads! What was this thing? Was it a virus?

"My scissors!" the leader of the seniors suddenly realised.

Anant had programmed his space-time-machine to do a simple task. It was all logical. The task was to move Anant through time as well as space. In round one, Anant had snatched the scissors. Then round two began a few seconds after round one and lasted an entire minute. In this minute, Anant was transported to the future for around 25 times. The future time to which he was transported on all those occasions was exactly the same but the space was different, but not by much. Anant tended to each senior five times. He had visualised how he would do it. He time-travelled to time t which was around one and a half minutes into the future and space s1, stayed there for a split-second in which he snipped off hair from a head came back to time t-90seconds, stayed her for 2 seconds, then time-travelled to time t again but at space s2, snipped off some more hair and returned to time t-88seconds, again stayed here for two seconds, and the process continued till the final time-travel was made to space s25, and he had still around half a minute before he could enjoy watching 25 versions of himself at work at the same time t. But it was just a blur or a wave that came and disappeared, and then the hair of the seniors started falling off in chunks.

"My scissors," said the leader of the ragging group again. "Where are they?"

"Your scissors did it?" asked Sheela. "That thing has a mind of its own?"

Anant looked at the scissors in his hand, but the next moment, they were in the leader's breast pocket. Round three now began, but it was not in auto-mode.

"There!" Sheela cried, pointing. "In your pocket."

The leader looked down at his pocket, and was about to pull his weapon out, when it just vanished. And then Sheela shrieked once again as she felt something in her shirt pocket. She looked down and saw the scissors, but didn't have the courage to touch them, nor could she have them there. That thing had a mind of its own. It was possessed! She looked at the senior leader pleading with her eyes to do something when that thing was suddenly no longer in her pocket. The juniors were unnerved too, but they were also enjoying what was happening to the ragging group. The scissors were now in the large boy's pocket who had stopped the younger Anant around three and half years ago. And now the vanishing object was back in Sheela's pocket yet again. Anant's subconscious mind had automatically made him do it. He realised it and decided that would be the last time. Pervert!- Anant scolded himself. She was indeed a part of the group on purpose- to humiliate the juniors more by her presence. But Anant had Sheela let off without her hair being shredded like the others. Anant didn't have the heart to snip off her hair. It would have been horrible to her. But now he had used her pocket twice, and it was not just with the intention of scaring her. So now he left her alone and the scissors were gone once again and ended up in another senior's pocket. The thing remained there, but the leader once again felt something being put inside his breast pocket. Looking down and realising that it wasn't that possessed thing, he put his hand in and took it out. It was a piece of paper. It had something written on it. He read it out aloud.

'Bend down on your knees and ask for forgiveness from your juniors. NOW! And if I ever find you ragging...'

The leader was terrified. He fell to his knees and said sorry to his juniors. Sheela followed and so did the rest of the seniors. The senior, who had the scissors in his pocket, now reluctantly managed to throw the possessed thing away.

Satisfied by what he had done, Anant looked at his watch. There was still time for his younger self to reach college. Anant had some information in his upgraded brain regarding how one cannot go back in time and meet one's younger self. It would be a paradox. Because the older Anant had no memory of his future self meeting him, it would create a paradox. But Anant doubted that it would really shake up space-time as some theories predicted. He knew that he, at the moment too, had created a paradox by erasing an episode from his own past. The younger Anant was not going to encounter the ragging group, and yet the older Anant still had the memory of his own encounter three years ago. That meant reality had not changed instantaneously. Maybe it could change once he got back to his own time because that would mean the completion of an event of time-travel. Or it may just happen that he would still have the memory of his own encounter. Anant doubted that his memory of the ragging episode from three years ago would just vanish when he returned to his timeline. He suspected that the memory would stay with him. And though he felt that the paradox theory was over-hyped, he was not going to test it further by meeting his younger self. He was not here for that. He clicked some buttons on his digital watch and vanished from the scene. He had reached his native timeline again. Looking at the wall clock, he felt reassured that from his timeline's perspective, he had never left it. He was back at the same time. No time had passed between the time he had gone to the past and the time he had returned here. He had set the watch on his machine to take him back to almost the exact time he had left his timeline. He had cheated time that day, for his day had been longer than twenty-four hours, if the time he had spent in the past had to be added to it. He smiled, wriggled himself out of his boiler suit... ...and then he staggered and fell on his knees. His head spun. He clutched it in his hands as images flashed in front of his eyes. He wanted to cry out aloud, but he didn't; he didn't want to wake up his parents. And so he crouched on the floor and lay there breathing ragged breaths.

The Change:

It was not unlike the day when Anant's brain was uploaded with the database by Prof. Wagh. Today too, new memories were added to Anant's brain. However, this process was natural. Anant had expected new memories would be added, but he hadn't expected it would be similar to that day at the institute. He had reckoned that there would be only a few new memories, but he had been wrong. There were so many of them that he had once again like that day at the institute, blacked out after the initial flashes in front of his eyes when he lay crouched on the floor. The blackout continued for a while, and then it automatically turned into sleep. He woke up late the next morning, but it was a Sunday. So, it was fine.

"Studied late into the night?" asked his mother.

"Yes. No. Yes," Anant replied; he was feeling disoriented and he was confused too and he was also confused about why he was feeling confused.

His father laughed.

"OK," he said. "Tell us when you are sure."

Anant smiled too, but he had to make a lot of effort for it. He better have his bath quickly. Didn't he have a date with Pooja? Pooja? Who's Pooja? My girlfriend. Yes, but the fact is I don't have a girlfriend. Anant froze. He thought hard. Did he have or did he not have a girlfriend? There were two sets of memories in his brain. These two sets existed only for the memories of the last three and a half years. One set said he had a girlfriend, and the other set said he didn't have one. Pooja, he thought. And one part of his brain said that she was his girlfriend, and the other part of his head didn't recognise this name as belonging to someone close. Pooja was in his college, his class. They were together for the last three years, and this was the fourth year. Anant then turned to the other set of memories, but this set didn't have any Pooja in it. Not only was he not friends with a girl called Pooja, but she was not in his college either. There was no such person that he knew of according to the other memory set. This was so odd. It was like watching two movies at the same time- two movies which had the same actors, but different storylines and dialogues. The memories came to him, but with some difficulty. *Pooja? Where is Pooja?*- he got desperate. Calm down; it's OK, he thought. Even if he didn't know her, he could go and meet her. But then she would not recognise him because they had never met. But why hadn't they met? They hadn't met because there was not such girl in his college. Then who were his friends? As he thought about it, he realised that there were some common names in both the memory sets. And there was one other name too, which was common in both sets, and in both sets, that name wasn't a friend. That name was much more than just an acquaintance, but it wasn't a friend. The name was Tejaswini. In the other newer memory set also, Tejaswini had been his crush since the first year. He had thought of her as extremely beautiful and out of his league. She was much simpler though in this new memory than in the original set, but Anant still hadn't had the guts to talk to her. He had known her to come from a rich family, and so he had stayed away, unable to express to her his interest in her. But Pooja too came from a rich family, didn't she? But he and Pooja were just friends initially. He had not intended on making her his girlfriend. It had just happened. But with Tejaswini, it wasn't so. He had a crush on her, and according to both memories, his intention hadn't ever been that of developing a friendship with her, but something more, and because he knew this, he never had the guts to talk to her. In one of the sets, he had known through Pooja that Tejaswini too had a crush on him, but in the other set, he knew no such thing for sure. He had sometimes caught her glancing at him, and sometimes becoming self-conscious in front of him, but he had attributed it to his own interest in her. He had thought that she had somehow known about his crush on her because of his own glances at her and that was the reason she became uncomfortable in his presence. How could a girl like that be interested in someone so average as him? This was their fourth year together in the same college in the same subject and yet they had never talked to each other. Anant realised that in this second memory set, Tejaswini had not left college or turned into a model. She was still there, and he saw her almost every day of the week.

"Why are you standing there in the middle of the room like a horse in its stable?" his father asked.

"He must have gone off to sleep," his mother commented.

"Just feeling confused," Anant replied.

"About what?"

"Nothing. Going for a bath," he said and hurried to the bathroom.

The interruption in Anant's thoughts brought his mind back to Pooja. When he had strayed and started thinking about Tejaswini, he seemed to have stuck there. Now, he again thought about Pooja. How come Pooja wasn't in his college? Then he tried to remember what had happened. In the original reality, Anant had stepped into the college, confronted the ragging group, reached his class late because of this and then he had sat at the first empty seat he had seen. This seat had been beside Pooja. In the second reality, because the older Anant had time-travelled and taken care of the ragging seniors, the younger had made it to his class on time. He had taken a seat in that half of the class which was away from the blackboard. He had taken a seat on an empty bench, and he had been alone there for the first lecture. There was no Pooja there or even later in all the three years of his graduation. Anant thought about it. He had time-travelled only three and a half years into the past. He couldn't have changed anything before that. Pooja obviously had taken admission in the college before that. So how could her not being in his college be a result of his time-travel? And yet, she wasn't there. He had thought that the paradoxes of time-travel were over-hyped. But was he wrong? He had time-travelled at least 25 times- in fact more than that- while he was in the act of time-travel. He had created smaller time-loops within a larger time-loop. And in that process, he had met his own time-travelling selves so many times- when he had snipped off the hair of the ragging group. But how could that have anything to do with Pooja not being in his college? Anant was correct in assuming the after-effects of time-travel. Some of the information that he had in his brain from the uploaded database said that time-travel would cause reality to change in such a way that the original reality would get erased. Anant agreed with that. That same theory said that the reality would change and the time-traveller would not have any memory of the original reality. But Anant had doubts about this. His logic said that the time-traveller would not forget the original reality. He was right; he hadn't lost any memories from the first reality. Well, if he had lost those memories, there wouldn't have been a way to tell, but since he had two sets of memories, he knew he had been correct. He would retain the memories of this first reality because he was in the time-loop. When he would travel to the past, reality would change, he had reckoned. But it would not change instantaneously. He would have to come back to his timeline for the second reality to take effect. He knew he was correct in this assumption as well. This is because while he was there in the past, he still had only one set of memories even while he was changing the past. The future did not change dynamically. The act of time-travelling back to his own timeline completed the act of 'observation'- in the Quantum Mechanics sense of the word- and only then reality changed. Till he had not returned to his timeline, the changed reality remained in existence only as a probability. It would collapse to a hard reality only after his return. Once he was back, the Anant in the time-loop and the Anant who had lived his life in the second reality would merge. The second reality would take effect for all the people including Anant. The others would not have any memory of the first reality because they were not a part of the time-loop, but Anant would remember the first reality also because he had brought about the change by being in the time-loop. He had been correct in all his speculations, but what he didn't know was how Pooja wasn't there in his college. He would have understood it, had she not been his girlfriend in the second reality, for minor changes in the past could end up manifesting as major changes of the present, but Pooja's not taking admission in their college stumped him. He would have had to go much further behind in the past to bring about that change and he hadn't done that. So how come...?

During lunch that day, Anant decided to ask his parents and verify his second set of memories.

"Do you know my friend called Pooja?" he asked.

"Pooja from your school?" his mother said.

"No. That was when I was in primary school so many years back. She was not my friend. She was a classmate just by the name Pooja."

"No then. You haven't told us anything about this new Pooja. What about her?"

"No. Nothing. She was there till last year in our college," he lied. "Now we have lost touch."

"OK then call her."

"Hmmm... I will."

His mother had just given him an idea. He would call her. But as he unlocked his phone, he wondered whether he would have her number still saved in his phone. The reality had changed, hadn't it? So if he did not know Pooja now, he shouldn't have her number. But then he had carried his phone during his time-travel and so this phone too was a part of the loop in time that he had created. So, logically, he should have her number. But did chip memory work the same as human memory in the time-loop? That wasn't the point at all. Anything that was a part of the time-loop would merge with the changed reality and if there was something from the original reality that did not exist in the second reality, it would still exist only because it was a part of the time-loop. And then it suddenly struck him. Logically, he was right. But he didn't need logic for that; he had the proof of this all the time with him. In the second reality, he hadn't met Pooja. Consequently, he hadn't met her father. As a result, he never had the database uploaded in his brain that he had through Prof. Wagh. And in absence of this data upload, the Anant in the second reality had never built a time-machine, and yet in this current reality, Anant had the time-machine with him. Thanks to the time-loop, it hadn't ceased to exist after his return to his timeline. He also realised that had the changes in the past been dynamic as some time-travel theories suggested, he would have lost his space-time-machine the moment he had reached the past, or at least sometime later, because the second reality didn't have the invention of the time-machine as a part of it. It was the legacy of the first reality that had stayed with him along with his first set of memories. Anant now clicked on the Contacts button of his phone. As expected, he found Pooja's number. Even if he hadn't found it, he had it by heart, but still he was glad to find it there on his phone. He almost clicked on the Call button, but stopped. Pooja didn't know him in this reality. What was he going to talk to her about? Well, he would at least hear her voice and ask for someone, and then apologise saying he had dialled a wrong number. He finished his lunch, washed his hands and then hit the Call button. He waited as the call got connected.

"Hello?" a gruff voice answered Anant's call.

It wasn't Pooja- obviously, not her mother- that too obviously, and her father didn't sound anything like the voice Anant now heard.

"Oh sorry," Anant said. "I think I dialled a wrong number."

Locking his phone, he scratched his head. Now he was getting restless. A few minutes later, he got dressed and stepped outside. He walked towards the institute. He lingered outside its gates. This was a Sunday. No one would be in. Moreover, how was he going to enter the premises? No one knew him there. He had never visited this place in the current reality. He looked at the building of the institute sadly and then started walking away. Now what? Not that coming to the institute was going to help him anyway. He wasn't going to meet Pooja there. He had come here just to check whether the institute existed. Now he had to take the risk of going to Pooja's place. No one knew him there too. So what? He had to try. This was the only way he could meet Pooja and win back her friendship and love. Oh! Love? How was he going to make her fall in love with him again? And what if she already had a boyfriend? What had he done? What had he done to himself? He had time-travelled and that had been a rash decision. He hadn't thought it through. He had miscalculated about the repercussions of time-travel, and now he had lost a major chunk of his life- that life which was going on smoothly. He walked slowly towards Pooja's house. He didn't know what he was going to say to her or her father or mother once he was there. No one was going to believe him. It would be the most ridiculous story he would tell them. But he had proof. He had the space-time-machine with him. But he was not going to show them that. And even if he showed them that, he could not prove anything unless he actually travelled in it again, and *that,* he wasn't going to do again- at least not until he found out how his time-travel to the past- three years ago- had changed something *before* that particular time. So what was he going to tell Pooja and her parents if he mentioned the time-machine? Maybe he would say that the time-machine vanished once he returned, and some of his data from his brain also got lost so that he could not remember how he had built the time-machine. Pooja's father still might believe him because Anant would tell him about Prof. Wagh and his experiment. Once he believed Anant, he could disclose that Pooja had been his girlfriend and if she believed it, it would not be long before they became friends again and she fell in love with him. But other factors remained- like her probable boyfriend. *Whatever-* thought Anant. He was going to her place and then he would decide what to say.

Anant rang the bell at Pooja's apartment. His heart thumped in his chest as he waited for the door to open. It opened. Pooja's father was standing in front of him. Looking at the familiar face, Anant almost smiled, but then he realised Pooja's father could not recognise him.

"I...," stammered Anant. "I have come to meet Pooja."

Pooja's father blinked as if startled and then he frowned, and stared at Anant.

"I think you have the wrong address," he said. "There is no Pooja here."

"Huh?" Anant said and he too blinked, shocked.

Pooja. Oh no. Pooja does not exist? Anant couldn't believe it. His heart sank. He wanted to just sit there on the floor and weep. But how could that happen? All this time, he had been thinking that Pooja hadn't taken admission in his college, but it had never crossed his mind that Pooja could not exist.

"Are you OK?" Pooja's father (or whoever else's father he was) asked, seeing the colour vanish from Anant's face.

"No," Anant said. "There is something wrong. I am confused, I think. It's unreal."

Pooja's father opened the door wider.

"Who do you want to see?" he asked, his voice soothing, trying to calm down Anant.

"Pooja."

"Surname?"

"Pooja Sathe."

"I think there is really some confusion. My surname is Sathe," he said and added, "Come in. Have some water. Come on, come in."

Anant went in and sat in the chair he had sat in twice before, but in that other reality. Pooja's father poured Anant a glass of water, and he gulped it down as if doing this would change something back to normal.

"What address do you have? Show me."

"I don't have it written down. I just know Pooja stays... stayed here."

"Coincidentally, my surname is Sathe. So, it might just be some misunderstanding."

"No."

"OK. Tell me; how do you know this Pooja?"

"She was in my college."

Pooja's father asked him about his college, and Anant told him the name of his college.

"I think there surely is some confusion," Pooja's father said, but his voice seemed distant as if he was distracted and was trying to figure out what Anant was confused about. "My daughter goes to the same college."

Anant looked up, surprised and now hopeful that Pooja's name might have changed in this reality.

"Oh. Can I see her? Maybe I am confused about her name."

"But you came to see Pooja. What was it about?"

"We lost touch, and she has perhaps changed her phone number. I just wanted to meet my friend," Anant knew all this would just seem very suspicious because there was no way a friend would forget a friend's name and drop by at her apartment asking for her.

Pooja's father looked at Anant, not able to decide. Then he suddenly turned and went inside one of the rooms, said something to someone and returned and sat down in front of Anant. From the periphery of his vision, Anant saw someone approaching him from that room- a girl. He looked up in her direction, and was so shocked, he jumped up and was on his feet.

"You?" he said, surprised.

The girl raised her eyebrows, but then she smiled at him. Anant blinked as if to make the girl in front of him disappear and bring Pooja back in her place, but this didn't help. The girl remained the same girl that she was.

"You know her?" the father of this girl sitting in front of Anant asked.

"Yes," Anant said. "She is Tejaswini."

Anant started thinking again. He tried to remember Tejaswini's name from this reality. Indeed it was Tejaswini Sathe. Then he tried to remember her name from the original reality. In that reality, she was Tejaswini Samant. That meant her father had changed.

"Anant, what are you doing here?" Tejaswini asked, but it was just a question; it wasn't a suggestion that he should leave.

"I came to see someone who I thought stayed here. And this was just a coincidence that her surname and your surname are the same. I must have really got confused. Should I see a doctor?" he said, directing the question at Tejaswini's father.

Anant had known this man as Pooja's father, and now it seemed weird to look at him as Tejaswini's father. But then where the hell was Pooja? And then it struck him. He remembered the time in the original reality when he had been waiting for Pooja and surfing on social media when he had come across Tejaswini's page where she had posted her model-like photos. Anant had seen her family photo as well. He had then seen her father- Mr. Samant. Anant had later searched about him on the internet. He was a celebrity-kind of. He was a director- an ad-filmmaker. Anant had then realised why Tejaswini had quit college after graduation and was trying to pursue a career in modelling. But that was not all. Anant had found out about Mr. Samant only later on. But when he had actually seen Tejaswini's family photo, he had noticed that she had inherited her looks from her mother. She looked a great deal like her mother. And if this Tejaswini standing in front of him right now looked the same as the Tejaswini from the original reality, it had to mean that her mother had remained the same. And that consequently meant that Pooja's mother was no longer Mr. Sathe's wife. Anant desperately wanted to see Tejaswini's mother now, but how was he going to say that? How would it appear if he were to ask them to meet her mother. Anant kept silent.

"Maybe," Tejaswini's father said.

"Huh?" Anant asked, confused.

"You asked whether you should see a doctor. But I don't know much about what your condition is. So I said maybe you require one."

"Oh that. Yes, I will see a doctor. I should leave. Tejaswini, I am sorry for all this. Hope you don't feel I have gone crazy."

"No. I just saw you yesterday in college. I didn't feel anything was wrong with you," she said.

"Thanks a lot," Anant said and turned to leave.

"Take care, Anant. I think you will be fine," Tejaswini said.

"Thank you again," Anant said, and felt a bit better at her kind words.

As he reached the door, however, he heard someone speak.

"Who was it?" Tejaswini's mother had just walked out into the hall.

Anant turned and looked at her. She was the same woman from the photo. Tejaswini looked like her mother.

"Sorry madam. It was me. There was some misunderstanding," Anant said to Tejaswini's mother.

She smiled at him and nodded. This woman at least looked a lot more approachable than Pooja's mother. Oh yes- Pooja's mother- Anant had to find her. Maybe, Pooja was still her daughter. He turned back and went out of the apartment.

As he walked home, Anant though hopeful that if he found Pooja's mother, he would find Pooja, he knew Pooja hadn't looked like her mother. She looked like a mixture of her father and mother. So even if Pooja's mother in this reality had a daughter called Pooja, she may not look the same as the Pooja he knew. And even if she looked like the original Pooja, she would not be that Pooja, in the same way that this Tejaswini wasn't the same Tejaswini from the original reality. She didn't have the same genes. She had a different father now. Anant had a feeling his search for Pooja was going to be futile, because not only did she look a mixture of her father and mother, but as a person, she was much like her father, and even if Pooja existed now, if Mr. Sathe was not her father anymore, what kind of Pooja's variant would she be? She might even be better, but who knew?

As soon as he reached home, Anant decided he was not going to go to college this week. He wanted to look for Pooja; moreover, it would be awkward to face Tejaswini. Until today, they hadn't talked to each other. Both knew the other existed, but neither had acknowledged each other's presence. But now, it would not be so. Now, whenever they came face to face, they would have to acknowledge each other, and for Anant, after what happened today at Tejaswini's place, this was going to be difficult. He would think about the awkwardness later. Right now, he wanted to look for Pooja's mother. Through her, he could find Pooja. So, what was Pooja's mother's name? He knew her name, but that wasn't going to help much. He didn't know her maternal surname. And even if he had known it, that wouldn't have been of much help either if she was now using her current husband's surname. Back to square one- how was Anant going to find Pooja's mother?

Where had she stayed before her marriage to Mr. Sathe in the previous reality? He didn't know that. What was her profession? He had never concentrated on Pooja's parents, though later he had come to know about where her father worked. But yes, he also knew her mother worked in a college. She was a professor. It was long back that Pooja had told him about her mother, when he and Pooja had only been friends. He had wondered why she had not taken admission in the same college where her mother worked, but that would have been awkward for both the mother and the daughter. Should he go tomorrow to that college and try to meet her? Anant knew he would seem even more ridiculous to Pooja's mother than he had seemed to Tejaswini and her parents of the current reality. Moreover, Pooja's mother had never been an approachable person. So what good would it do to meet her? She would never tell a total stranger about her own daughter- that is, if she had one. So what now? Was there another approach to the situation? Hmmm... Tejaswini's mother? But he didn't know anything about her from the old or the new reality except that she was the wife of Mr. Samant- the ad-filmmaker. He was a celebrity then. He could be a celebrity now. Information about him could be more easily available, Anant realised. So, he started searching the internet for Samant- the ad-maker. It didn't take long. Samant was an ad-film director in this reality too. He was not married, but he was not single either. An article about him said he had remained single in his youth. Now he was in a live-in relationship with a model who was around 15 years younger than him. He didn't have a child. OK, thought Anant. He wasn't expecting Pooja to be his daughter in this reality just because Mr. Sathe was now Tejaswini's father. Reality would have changed based on some logic, and not changed just by swapping the parents of Pooja and Tejaswini. But how come Mr. Sathe married Tejaswini's mother? The two girls whom he had liked- reality had changed for those same two girls. How?- that he didn't know. But now thinking on those lines, he suddenly felt as if Pooja and Tejaswini were one and the same girl in this reality. Pooja was likeable because she was her father's daughter. Tejaswini was likable because she was her mother's daughter. Pooja had her father's good nature. Tejaswini too perhaps had inherited her mother's good nature- Anant was speculating this as he could not have been sure- and her mother's looks. Now, through Mr. Sathe and Tejaswini's mother, Pooja and Tejaswini had merged to become one person. This merging, though on the surface looked similar to how the Anant from the original reality had merged with the Anant of the second reality, it was quite different as neither Pooja and

Tejaswini had been a part of the time-loop. Anant was speculating on whether Pooja and Tejaswini had become one person, but he still wasn't sure whether Pooja existed or not in this current reality. He sighed. Meeting Pooja's mother, though possible, was not a feasible option. So, the other option was that he could ask Tejaswini how her father and her mother met and then on the basis of that information, try to find out where to look for Pooja. But to talk to Tejaswini, he would have to meet her, and for that he would have to go to college, but hadn't he just decided that he was not going to go to college this week? Well then, he would have to.

VI

Anant and Tejaswini:

Anant went to college the next day- Monday. The thought of meeting Tejaswini made him feel quite nervous. He would have to find some excuse to talk to her. Eager to reach college and talk to her made him reach there early and he went and sat on one of the benches towards the back. If he had to have any information from Tejaswini, he would have to tell her the truth, as absurd it may sound, because there wasn't a lie that would not sound even more absurd. He reckoned he would have to confide in her. He found himself fidgeting- shaking his leg- in anticipation of the day and his conversation with Tejaswini ahead of him. Some girls now entered the class. He recognised them from his second set of memories as being the group of which Tejaswini was a part. But she hadn't come yet. He had some friends too- those who were not a part of the original reality, but none of them was there yet. It was still a bit early. He waited, his eyes on the door. And then she entered- Tejaswini. Anant's leg suddenly stopped shaking. Whatever decision he had made until now, seemed to have dissolved and disappeared from his mind. Looking at her and thinking what she must think of him after yesterday made him forget what he was going to say. This was going to be a very difficult task. He had encouraged himself by saying that he would find a way to talk to her and confide in her the truth, but he didn't have a clue how he was going to do that, and now that he saw her there in the class, he just wanted to run away and get home. Why the hell did he come here today? Tejaswini directly looked at the place where her friends usually sat. She automatically turned towards them, but then she slowed down and glanced around. She saw him. Uh-oh, thought Anant, who didn't know how to react. He slightly nodded his head in her direction as an acknowledgement. She glanced back at her friends, and mouthed 'Later'; she then turned and started walking in his direction. He was terrified of facing her. He again had this urge and it even was stronger than the previous one- he just wanted to get up and run away. The current reality had taken some more control of his mind now, and in this reality, she still had a huge crush on her, and this along with what happened yesterday totally unnerved him as she approached him. But he stayed there anchored to his place just because running away would look extremely ridiculous and he didn't want to look like a fool in front of her again.

"Hi," she said.

"Mind if I sit here? I know maybe one of your friends may join you, but just for this lecture, is it OK?"

"Ye... yes. Sure. Please," he said, stammering.

She smiled and sat beside him as her group giggled. She glared at them, and the giggles got somewhat stifled.

"How are you?" she asked.

"I... I am feeling OK. Thanks."

"Did you find your friend?"

He was tense and his hands had gone cold. Calm down- he said to himself.

"Er... This may sound odd," he said, "but I may require your help."

"My help?" she said, not knowing how she was going to help him find *his* friend.

"I said it may sound odd, and it did, didn't it?"

"No. I am just surprised because I don't even know your friend. I am not judging you," her voice was so soothing and she sounded so sincere that Anant became a bit relaxed.

"Thanks. I want to tell you... er... talk to you about a few things."

"Do you want to skip this lecture to talk?"

"I can," Anant said, "but I wouldn't want you to miss it for me."

"I don't mind. Let's go."

"Are you sure?"

"I can study theory from any book. I wouldn't want to miss the practicals though."

"OK," he said.

Tejaswini stood up and started towards the door. Anant took his bag and followed.

"Tejuuuuu...," someone from her group cried out, and the rest of her friends giggled.

Tejaswini looked at them with an annoyed look on her face, but she was trying to suppress an embarrassed smile and her cheeks had gone very red. She swiftly moved out of the classroom.

Once outside the classroom, Tejaswini didn't look at Anant for some time, neither did she say anything. She was still very embarrassed and didn't want him to see her blushing. Once they reached the staircase, she turned to him.

"Want to go down or...?"

"Canteen?" he suggested.

"Yes. Good idea."

The canteen was quite empty at this time.

"Do you want to have anything?" she said as they placed their bags down finding a table at a corner.

"No."

"Me neither. So... we will just sit here."

"Yes."

They both sat down facing each other, and Anant realised he now had to actually tell her a lot of unbelievable things. She looked at him expectantly.

"I don't know whether I will be able to complete this in forty-five minutes."

"Don't worry about the lectures," she said, "unless you want to attend them. We have three hours until the practicals."

Anant smiled.

"Thanks," he said.

"You can say thanks at the end of three hours," she said and smiled a good-natured smile at him.

"What I want to tell you will sound..."

"Odd?" she asked.

"Extremely," he replied.

"Then I am even more curious to know what it is that you have to say."

"You have a knack of making people comfortable when they are feeling exactly the opposite," he said, impressed.

She smiled a bit shyly.

"I am an average student...," he began.

"No, you are not. You are quite smart," she said, interrupting him. "I have seen your marks in the last three years."

"You have?" he asked, surprised, for he had also been checking out her marks on the notice board, and this, he knew, was just like the original reality.

She had blurted out this little secret without thinking, and now her eyes widened as she was racking her brain to think about an excuse or something on those lines. Anant was looking at her and wondering whether she, in this reality too, had a crush on him. Had she glanced at him from time to time because she was interested in him? He had always assumed that she had done that because she suspected him to have a crush on her.

"Yes, I have," she said, not able to think of any excuse or any other thing to say.

"OK," he said with the intention of continuing with what he wanted to tell her. "I meant I considered myself not a lot above-average until yesterday. No, wait. For you it can be yesterday. For me, it was sometime earlier this year."

Tejaswini looked at him, confused.

"Sorry. I might say such things. Just don't think I am crazy because though I suggested yesterday that I might be going mad, there is really nothing wrong with me. I just don't know how to tell you an unbelievable story."

"As I said yesterday," she said, "I don't feel anything is wrong with you. So don't worry about it. Tell me everything as it is because if you worry about how it may sound, you may try to modify some things to make them less weird, and then it will not be the truth."

"I told you, you have a knack, and I was right. So here it is. But first, let me tell you that I consider myself much above average for the last few months. I am not being modest and it is because it would be a lie. I became smart because I was a part of this experiment...," and then Anant stopped abruptly as he started to think about the experiment.

Did the experiment happen in this reality too? The Anant of the second reality was unaware of it, but that was because Pooja wasn't his friend here, and Tejaswini was Pooja's father's daughter. *How much more ridiculous was that going to get?- he thought as he called Tejaswini- Pooja's father's daughter.* But because he didn't know Mr. Sathe in this reality until yesterday, he couldn't have been called as a candidate for the test. If he wasn't the one who was selected in this reality, who was it? In the original reality, they hadn't found any other suitable candidate. So it was possible that they hadn't found anyone in this reality too. And perhaps the experiment still waited to be conducted on a human. Or was it that they had found someone in Anant's absence, and they had conducted the test on that person? And this person might...

"Anant?" Tejaswini called him.

"Sorry. I... I think your father may have a lot of answers for the questions I have."

"What? How?"

"I know it's already becoming unbelievable for you. So, fine. I will demonstrate something. Ask me to multiply or divide some randomly large numbers and keep your calculator ready to verify."

Tejaswini looked at Anant, confused, but she obliged. She asked him to do some random calculations, and each time, she was surprised at how fast he gave the answers without even thinking for a second. In fact, he answered her before she could type in the numbers- and she was doing this simultaneously as she said the numbers aloud- and clicked on the 'equal to' sign to display the answer.

"How? But how does this prove that you were a part of any experiment? There are people with such capabilities."

"You are right," he agreed. "But think logically. If I had been great at numbers right from my childhood, wouldn't I already be famous? At least I would have been famous in our college. Or think, why would I have taken biology- wouldn't have I taken mathematics as my subject for graduation?"

"True," Tejaswini said as she didn't have an answer to his questions.

"Now you can ask me anything on any subject. I will answer it if I have that information. And yes, there is a high probability that I might know the answer."

So she asked him how many moons Jupiter had, and he answered that correctly. Which was the nearest galaxy to our own Milky Way galaxy? He answered that too. The nearest star apart from our sun? The distance of Earth from this star? Number of stars in our galaxy? Size of the universe? Age of the universe?

"Why astronomy?" he asked.

"Sorry. I asked the first question in astronomy and then I just got carried away," she laughed. "OK. Fine. I believe you. Now continue with your story. But by the way, what is the radius of the Earth?"

"Shut up!" he said and they both laughed.

"Continue," she urged him.

But how was he to tell her that she was not her father's daughter in the reality from which he had come? It would be shocking to her. How would she take the fact that her mother was married to a different man? Mr. Samant...

"Tejaswini? Do you happen to know a person called Prof. Wagh?"

"Yes. I have heard of him from my father. But how do you...?"

"I will come to that. And what about an ad-film director called Samant?"

"Oh. I know him too. I have even met him once or twice. He used to stay near my mother's place. Her maternal place, I mean."

OK, thought Anant. So Tejaswini's mother in the first reality had married an ad-maker, Samant who stayed near her place.

"How did your mother and father meet?"

"Why are you asking questions about my parents and how do you know the people I know?" she asked suspiciously.

"You have again started not believing me."

"Has that experiment made you a clairvoyant or something? Are you reading my mind?"

"No."

"Then?"

"I come from a world where I used to know your father."

"What are you talking about?"

"Tejaswini, I can't go on without telling you something that will shock you."

"What is it?"

"I cannot tell you this until you promise me that this will remain only between the two of us."

"What is it?" she was now getting impatient.

"You promise me or I will not go on," Anant said, matching the sternness in her voice.

Tejaswini considered. She was intelligent, and being intelligent made her curious. And curiosity now controlled her more than her suspicions about Anant.

"OK. I promise," she said finally.

"But how do I know you will keep your promise?"

"That you can't. You will have to trust me."

"I guess I have to do that," he said and started his story.

Anant told Tejaswini how he had met Pooja. She was in the same class as he was. And then they became the best of friends. Then one day, Pooja had told him about a girl who was interested in him and then when it seemed to her that he too liked her, Pooja had become jealous and that was when she had realised she had fallen in love with Anant. Anant too had later accepted to become her boyfriend.

Tejaswini till now had kept quiet, but now she stopped Anant.

"What are you saying? We were in the same class and there was no one by the name Pooja in our college. Are you just imagining things or are you trying to make me jealous by saying that you had a girlfriend?"

"Why would you be jealous?" Anant asked.

"Ha... As if you don't know. Why do you think my friends were teasing me when I just left our classroom with you?"

"Wouldn't that have happened if you had left with any other boy? Are you trying to say that you like me?"

"Yes. I liked you- *liked*- in the past tense. And that's because right now, I don't know what you are or what you are getting at."

"You like me? OK. *Liked* me? But I always thought that you were out of my league. I didn't consider myself deserving of you. That's why I never approached you even when I liked you so much."

At this, Tejaswini's expression softened.

"OK," she said. "Complete your story."

And so Anant continued with Pooja's story and how her father had then asked them to take that test, and how he had got selected. With the knowledge he had now, Anant had built a machine, and with that machine, he had done nothing but to go back three years into the past and stop a ragging group. He told Tejaswini about how he had snipped off the hair of the seniors.

"But I haven't heard of this story," said Tejaswini. "Wouldn't something like that have spread throughout the college?"

"I too do not remember that as a part of my second memory set. So, that too like some other things prior to it, got erased or changed. There is no memory of me encountering the ragging group in my second memory set."

Tejaswini thought about the entire story that Anant had told her until now.

"You didn't mention a few names," she said. "Like who was Pooja's father. Or like who the scientist was who conducted the experiment. And I feel you left them out on purpose."

"That can be a difficult part for you to accept," he said.

And now Anant told her that when he had returned to his timeline, the reality had changed. Pooja was no longer there. He had memories from both the realities, and Pooja wasn't his girlfriend in this reality. He had come to Tejaswini's place yesterday looking for Pooja.

Tejaswini looked aghast. She couldn't say anything. How could a person imagine all this? So this might be all true. But how could such a thing happen? It was all too far-fetched to be true. Her mind couldn't accept the implications of Anant's story.

"You mean Pooja was my parents' daughter? Is that what you mean?"

"Not exactly. But she was your father's daughter."

"So who was her mother?"

"Pooja's mother wasn't your mother."

"But then you have also asked me about some things related to my mother."

"Yes. You existed in my previous reality too. You were the girl Pooja became jealous about. Your mother was the same, but your father was..."

"Samant?" Tejaswini asked.

"Yes."

"Huh?" Tejaswini was shocked even though she herself had guessed correctly who her father from the other reality was.

Anant gave her time to digest what she had just heard.

"And the scientist who conducted the experiment was Prof. Wagh?" she asked, even as she tried to recover from her shock.

"Correct."

"When did this experiment happen in your reality?"

"Three months after our post-graduation term started."

"But I have not heard of anything like that," she said. "I mean, if those two realities that you talk about have any similarities..."

"That's what I was thinking when I said that your father may have answers to my questions."

"But he doesn't know you in this reality, does he?"

"No, I don't think he knows me, but he may be able to shed some light on many things."

"But I don't get it. If you went only three years back in time, how did something much earlier than that get changed?"

"Exactly. But I think I may have some idea about how that happened," Anant said and added, "So, you believe me?"

"I haven't said that. Your story is highly imaginative and intelligent- I can give you full marks for that, but it is totally unbelievable. I admit you have intrigued me, but that doesn't mean I believe what you said. You are either totally out of your mind, but being able to imagine such a story may rule that out though not completely, or you are just up to something very criminal."

"I can't blame you for not believing me even after I answered all your questions on astronomy and maths correctly."

"Oh that," Tejaswini said, considering Anant's remarkable feat and knowledge. "I really don't know what to believe."

"Can we talk to your father?"

"I... I don't know. I mean you can talk to my father, but I don't know whether I want to be a part of it."

"I understand."

Tejaswini frowned, perhaps thinking about something.

"So, I am Pooja and Tejaswini both?" she asked suddenly, her eyes going wild.

"I cannot be sure until there is proof that Pooja does not exist in this reality, but from whatever we know about this reality, it seems that you are."

"If all this that you have told me is true, it seems you have just lost your girlfriend."

"From one perspective, yes. From another, no."

Tejaswini looked at Anant, stared at him, but not angrily. She knew what he meant. Then she blinked and looked away.

"I had asked you something, but at that time, you didn't answer,* Anant said.

"What?"

"How did your father and mother meet each other?"

"They were in the same college..."

Some Other Place: Some Other Time (Revisited):

The students had gone home one by one after completing their experiments for that day. Krishna was now alone with Lalita in the biology lab. He looked at her and cursed his luck. She would have to tolerate being with her for the rest of the evening. She was arrogant, and that's why he couldn't stand her, but otherwise, he didn't know much about her. Mostly she didn't talk much- at least not to him. So, it wouldn't be that difficult to be with her this evening, he thought. The centrifuge was running. Krishna and Lalita were going to wait till it stopped running. Then they would complete the experiment and leave for the day. Krishna slumped down in his chair while reading a book and dozed off. Lalita looked at him disapprovingly, but then a few minutes later, she too dozed off, her head on the table.

The security guard in the small cabin at the gate of the college looked at his watch. Everyone must have left. He would have to go and lock all the classrooms and the laboratories. He took the bunch of keys from the drawer, and came out of the cabin.

"Excuse me," said someone behind him, and the security guard turned to see a middle-aged man approach him.

"Yes?" said the security guard.

"Please give this to Prof. Krishna from the biology department when you are up there," the man said, handing over a sealed envelope to the guard.

"No. Everyone has gone home."

"No. Prof. Krishna and Prof. Lalita are in the biology lab. They will leave late after finishing their experiment. He had called me; that's why I know.

"Who are you? What should I tell him- who gave this letter?"

"I was in this college years ago. You don't need to tell him anything. He will know."

The security guard shrugged, and left with the envelope in his hand. Since he had the letter to deliver, he directly went to the biology lab before closing the classrooms. He opened the door, but didn't see anyone inside. So he walked inside, and then he saw them. Prof. Krishna was sleeping slumped into his chair, and Prof. Lalita with her head on the table. The security guard was grateful to the man who had just given him the letter. If that middle-aged man hadn't told him that the two professors were inside the lab, he would have locked it thinking no one was here. They weren't visible from the door. The guard approached the table and placed the envelope underneath Krishna's book. He didn't wake him up. He turned around and left to close the classrooms.

The centrifuge stopped. Krishna woke up, and saw the letter. It had his name on it. He opened it.

'You should ask her out someday. The earlier the better,' Krishna read this and was shocked, as he looked up at Lalita sleeping with her head down on the table.

What?- Krishna thought- ask this one out? But then he looked down at the letter again.

'Oh no,' it said, 'not the one you are with right now. I am referring to the other one. Stop thinking too much about what might happen. Just give yourselves a try. Trust me. She is older than you- so what?'

Krishna blinked. How did this person know about Supriya? Who was he... or she...? Krishna looked back at the letter. It said that later on he should try to get out of the college and become a research scientist. The letter also mentioned the name of an institute. Krishna was surprised. Was it Supriya who had written this letter to him so that he would ask her out? He would have liked that, but the institute and all- didn't seem like Supriya. He looked at the handwriting. It looked oddly familiar. It was like his own. Krishna frowned. The letter gave him a good piece of advice. So why not try it? What harm would it do? Supriya might say no, or she just might even accept to go out with him. OK, he decided, I will try to ask her in the next few days. He folded the letter and kept it in his pocket. He then stood up and walked towards the centrifuge. The thought about who could have written this letter lingered in his mind for a few minutes. Well, he may find that out, or he may not. As the letter said- don't think too much. And then his thoughts went back to his crush- Supriya.

Anant and Mr. Sathe:

Tejaswini decided this was something much more important than the practicals. So she and Anant walked home- Tejaswini's home. But her father wouldn't be home at this time. They would wait. The practicals might have taken long to finish, and she didn't have the patience to wait until then. Moreover, she wouldn't have been able to concentrate at all. So better wait at home for her father to return. Though initially she wasn't sure whether she wanted to be there when Anant and her father talked, she was now eager to be a part of the conversation. Curiosity! It would be awkward for her to be the part of a conversation in which Anant might tell her father that he was married to someone else, and now thinking about this, Tejaswini again felt unsure that she was doing the right thing- to bring along this boy who might seem to be completely insane to her family. He had appeared so yesterday and today she was bringing him home! She looked sideways at Anant, who was walking with her, lost in thought. And for a moment or two, she forgot all that he had told her. She just basked in the fact that she was walking home with her crush- she had liked this boy so much. For the past three years, she had been eyeing him up, but she never had the courage to talk to him. He was handsome; he was intelligent and he always behaved so decently with everyone. She had given up on the idea that something could ever materialise between them. She had given up long back, and had even virtually stopped thinking about him- virtually, because she used to see him every day. But she had learned to ignore her feelings. And now, all of a sudden, he was there beside her. Oh- how much I like him! Then, as suddenly as she had forgotten the circumstances, they came back to her. I just hope- she thought- he is telling the truth. I just wish he doesn't appear crazy to my father.

Anant and Tejaswini reached her apartment. She placed the key into the keyhole and turned. The key turned, but the door did not open. She frowned.

"It is locked from the inside. Someone's home," she said and rang the doorbell.

Mr. Sathe opened the door, looking as if he had been asleep. Oops- thought Anant- wrong timing. Tejaswini too thought the same.

"You returned early?" she asked her father.

"Never went. I almost got ready to go in the morning, but I wasn't feeling that good. So, stayed back. Hi there," he said to Anant.

"Are you fine? Fever?" Tejaswini asked before Anant could return his greeting.

"No fever. I am fine. Just tired. Come in now. Are you going to stand there?"

Anant and Tejaswini went in, but Anant stayed back at the door.

"I had come to talk to you," he said, "but I will come back later."

"Hmmm...," Tejaswini's father didn't seem to be able to decide.

"Bye, Tejaswini," Anant said and got out of the apartment.

"I am sorry," she said apologetically.

"But you can come with me if you want," he said. "We can just make it for the practicals."

Tejaswini couldn't decide. She could attend the practicals and she could be with Anant for some more time, but at the same time, her father was not well. So, should she stay home?

"He doesn't seem fine," she said. "I will stay."

Her father was just going to say to her that she could go if she wanted to, but before he could say anything Anant spoke to her.

"He will be OK. He just hasn't completed his sleep. He couldn't sleep after meeting me yesterday."

Tejaswini was completely startled at Anant's statement. It seemed very rude of him, she thought, and she had totally not expected it.

"How can you...?" she said, but she was interrupted by her father.

"You seem to be overconfident about my condition," he said to Anant.

"No, I am not overconfident. I am just sure," Anant said, but his voice was calm.

"Anant, you can't talk to my father like that."

"I am talking to Pooja's father; you just happen to be his daughter."

"Call him in," Tejaswini's father said to her. "We don't want our neighbours to gossip about some non-existent issue."

"You are inviting him in?" she asked her father incredulously, but before her father could reply, Anant had already got inside and closed the door.

Tejaswini had never seen this side of Anant. Anant also rarely saw this side of himself. It was only in special circumstances like this one or like the ragging episode that Anant suddenly turned aggressive. Now that he had entered the apartment again, the three of them looked at one another not knowing what to say.

"Now that you are here, say what you want to say," Tejaswini's father said.

"Tejaswini told me that you and her mother were in the same college."

"What? What is this about? Is it about the same thing as yesterday because if it is, I don't know what you are talking about."

"I have a theory," Anant said. "It says that an experiment was performed on you by one Prof. Wagh from your institute."

Tejaswini frowned. What was Anant talking about? Oh no- Anant really needed help. His mind was actually unstable! His rudeness was just a result of his condition. He was now confusing what he thought happened to him with her father. Even after Anant had demonstrated his prowess to her, his story itself was so unbelievable that she tended to incline quickly towards her suspicion that he was crazy, whenever he said something that she didn't understand.

"Anant," she said soothingly, "my father works in a research institute. He will be able to help you. Prof. Wagh, I have heard, is very good. He will help with your condition."

Anant looked at her and smiled. Tejaswini became all the more sure that he was indeed crazy, but his smile wasn't a crazy smile at all. It was a patronising smile.

"Tejaswini," he said, "I know Prof. Wagh. He has already helped me a lot," he now looked at Mr. Sathe.

Mr. Sathe looked confused. Looking at him, it appeared to Anant that he had been trying to figure out all night how Anant had known about Pooja, but he hadn't been able to solve the mystery. And it wasn't his shortcoming. Anant knew he himself wouldn't have been able to do it, had he been in Tejaswini's father's place. But from where Anant stood in the current situation, he thought of it as a vantage point from which he could see what had happened. He was still not sure, but well- almost.

"What are you trying to say? You know Prof. Wagh?" Mr. Sathe asked Anant.

"No. Not now, but once I did. But you changed it all. Where is your machine?"

"Which machine?"

"But why did you do it? Didn't you like Pooja- your own daughter?" Anant said, but it was only to provoke his opponent; he was quite confident that wasn't the reason.

"You should leave," he suddenly looked angry.

"Why are you suddenly so angry? I have lost my girlfriend. I should be the one to be angry, and yet I am calmer than you. Did you do it because Pooja wasn't intelligent enough to be your daughter?"

Mr. Sathe was now furious; it showed on his face, but he just kept quiet. Tejaswini noticed her father was angry, and she thought it was uncharacteristic of him. If he thought Anant was crazy, he wouldn't have been angry; he would have stayed calm and tried to convince Anant to go with him to the institute or to see a doctor. She now felt inclined to believe in Anant's story and in his theory. Anant was alleging that her father had changed something in his own past. That meant her father too had a time-machine, and that in turn implied that he too, like Anant...

"Wait. Wait you two," she said, showing them that she was trying to meditate. "I have a doubt."

Both Anant and Mr. Sathe looked at her.

"What would I be left with if I were to equally share some 62782 apples among 44389 men?"

"18393," said both Anant and her father at the same time.

Tejaswini looked at her father who stared back at her, then closed his eyes as he realised he had been caught, and shook his head. Anant smiled faintly at Tejaswini, impressed by her presence of mind.

"I hadn't asked that question to you," she said to Anant.

"Yes, I now know, but..."

"But even if you had known, you wouldn't have been able to stop yourself from answering it, because that stuff is ingrained in your brain. To answer a question like that has become your instinct, and that's why my father too answered it without thinking why I was distributing apples among men- so many apples among so many men- and that too when the two of you were having a fight. Right?" she asked her father, and added, "We better sit down now and start talking calmly to one another."

"But how did you guess that we would reply to such an absurd question?" Anant asked, as they all settled down in chairs.

"It wasn't a guess; I had observed this while you were flaunting your capabilities some time back in college."

"That was smart," Tejaswini's father said. "But you went against your own father."

"That- I did. But I want to know what this is all about. And would you have liked me thinking Anant is crazy when he is not?"

"OK. Fine. You got me there, but I don't really have any answers to Anant's questions. I don't know him though he seems to know me. And I have not figured out how. So it seems to me that he has the answers, not me."

"No," said Anant, "though I think I have figured out some things, those are only logical guesses. I have some questions. To begin with, I want to know whether Pooja exists in this reality."

"Yes and no. Yes, because Tejaswini is Pooja in this reality. She looks different because... you already know that."

"You don't know a lot of things. Tejaswini and Pooja both existed in my original reality."

"What?"

"Wait. You won't know what I am talking about. So, we will come to that later."

"I wanted to know whether Pooja exists in this reality as in what happened to Prof. Lalita," Anant said, and Mr. Sathe looked uncomfortably at Tejaswini.

"Lalita," Krishna Sathe said, "was my wife from another reality. She is now married to someone her parents married her off to."

"Does she have a daughter?" Anant enquired.

"No. I looked her up once the reality changed. She has a son, and he doesn't look like Pooja."

"OK," said Anant, devoid of emotion, "Tejaswini, you are officially both Pooja and Tejaswini."

"How? I mean I thought she was Pooja, but how can she be both?" asked Tejaswini's father, Krishna.

"Here's my story."

Anant began his story. He told him about how Pooja was his girlfriend, and how being her father, Mr. Sathe had told them both about Prof. Wagh's experiment and the volunteers that were required. Only he got selected. His brain was uploaded with a huge database. This knowledge and information finally led him to invent a space-time-machine, which he used to go into his past. He went three years into the past. He changed something. He thought it was a very minute change, but looking at the current reality, it apparently wasn't.

"I stopped the ragging group before my younger self entered the college on his first day. Now what happened after that, *that*- I can only guess because though that was a part of your original reality, you cannot possibly know about it. I don't know about it the same way you don't know about my original reality. So, here it is. I stopped the ragging group. Now, my younger self possibly entered college and directly went to his class. In my original reality, which you cannot remember now because you were not a part of the time-loop I created during my time-travel, I had ended up late in class because of the ragging and this had made me find the nearest empty seat and that happened to be beside Pooja. But now since the ragging was taken care of, I must have got into the class and sat on an empty bench or beside someone else other than Pooja; again, I can never know exactly what happened. I will call your original reality as my interim reality. My original reality was the cause for all this. So in a way, it preceded your original reality or my interim reality. And now my second reality and your second reality are the same. So, coming back to the story- since I didn't sit beside Pooja on the first day, we might not have become close friends- we may have remained acquaintances, and ultimately I did not end up being her boyfriend. Our friendship in my first reality had started to take shape right on the first day, and our not being together on the first day in the interim reality could cause such an effect- I had not been able to predict that. Now when Prof. Wagh tried to find his candidates, you must have asked Pooja to appear for the test. She must have failed just like in my reality."

"Yes. She failed," said Krishna, "and so did all the candidates. We couldn't find a suitable person for the experiment."

"Yes," said Anant. "You didn't know me and I possibly didn't come to know about the experiment. So I never turned up for the test. You didn't find anyone. Now, in my original reality, you had mentioned to me that Prof. Wagh wanted you to be the subject of the experiment, but you had denied. And when I got selected, the experiment was performed on me. But in your original reality, you didn't find any suitable candidate, and Prof. Wagh might have finally convinced you to become the subject."

"Yes, he did," said Krishna.

"So now, in that reality, your brain was uploaded with the database. Did you ask for any specific data? In my reality, I had requested you to ask Prof. Wagh if he could do it. Did you too?"

"Yes," replied Krishna. "I was already a biologist. So I told him to upload physics and chemistry."

"You too...? I did exactly the same thing."

"You two," said Tejaswini, "are quite similar, I think."

Anant smiled.

"So," he continued, "now that you had so much knowledge in your brain, you automatically started speculating and theorising, and then one day, you must have also built a time-machine. I would like to see that, but that's for later."

"You two really have time machines," said Tejaswini. "This is unbelievable. And this is awesome."

"Perhaps, you will not think it is awesome when Anant here completes his story," said Krishna.

"You too went into the past and changed something," said Anant. "Well, I have a guess here too. And please forgive me for being so bold to say it aloud in front of your daughter. You were not in love with your wife- I am referring to Prof. Lalita. Am I saying...?"

"You are right," Krishna admitted. "But did I in your reality say anything that would have suggested it?"

"No, not directly. You were always supportive of me. She wasn't. Moreover, I myself felt she wasn't that approachable."

"She is arrogant. She is OK, but she is arrogant. She never behaved arrogantly with me, but she did it with most other people. And I hate arrogance and arrogant people. She was my wife and the mother of my daughter. So I put up with her. My marriage to her," Krishna said this, now looking at Tejaswini, "was not out of my love for her, but circumstances had compelled it on both of us. My choice was your mother- Supriya, and I couldn't have been Lalita's natural choice either. So I just went back in time and nullified the circumstances that had led to our marriage."

Tejaswini seemed sympathetic towards her father because he had married and stayed in the marriage with the woman he was not in love with, but also had in fact disliked a part of her nature. But then Tejaswini's expression suddenly changed, and she frowned angrily at her father.

"How could you do it?" she said. "Pooja was your daughter. You may find me boring someday and then you will go back and...," she glared at her father.

Krishna looked at Anant for help.

"Why are you looking at him?" she asked her father.

"Tejaswini," said Anant, "imagine yourself to be in a relationship with a person who you know you cannot love, and especially when the person you like is somewhere nearby. You see him, but can't do anything about it. Given a chance, would you not undo your relationship with the person you don't love?"

Tejaswini thought about it. Though there wasn't anyone who she disliked, she too had gone through something like this. She had seen Anant every day at college for more than three years and she had wanted to be with him so much. Thinking about her situation and relating it to her father's, now the anger on her face dissolved.

"OK," she said, "I think I understand," and then all of a sudden, she stood up, angry again. "No," she said, "I don't understand. He murdered Pooja."

"What?" said Krishna and Anant in unison.

"You murdered her," she repeated.

"You cannot murder someone who does not exist," said Anant calmly.

Tejaswini looked at Anant incredulously.

"OK. Fine," Anant said. "I said that only for the sake of argument. But it's logical and true. No one murdered anyone here. But if you find that unbelievable, let me remind you- and you had come to the conclusion yourself- you are both Pooja and Tejaswini."

"No," she argued. "You said that I existed as Tejaswini in your reality."

"Yes, but that Tejaswini was different. A bit different."

"So he murdered that Tejaswini too."

Anant now chuckled, and Tejaswini looked at him, totally surprised.

"Realities merged for me and your father when we time-travelled. You are a product of those merged realities. You have the qualities of Pooja. You are less of a model and by that I don't mean you are less beautiful than the Tejaswini of my original reality. You look the same. I mean, in this reality, you are more down to earth than the Tejaswini I knew. I have to admit I didn't know her much, but I don't know you either, and yet I can spot the differences. You have Pooja's hair. Tejaswini had her black hair. You have dark brown hair like your father's. You are a mixture of the two and you are... you at least seem better than both the girls I knew. You are smarter than Pooja and slightly a better person than Tejaswini. It is from the vibes that I get from you that I say this, but I admit I may be wrong."

But even before Anant had said the last sentence, listening to him praise her, Tejaswini's cheeks had already gone a bit red, but she was not bowing down to Anant's logic.

"But my father didn't stay committed. I can understand he didn't like his wife, but he didn't stay committed to his daughter."

"I tried to remain committed," Anant said, "with Pooja. I had agreed to be her boyfriend because she was my best friend, and I didn't want her to get hurt. I liked her no doubt and I loved her too, but I hadn't *fallen in love* with her. I had always liked Tejaswini," he said and he stopped abruptly as he realised he had said it in front of Mr. Sathe and had also admitted to Tejaswini that in his original reality too, he had liked her. Well- he had told her that already when they had been talking in the canteen, but at that time, he had just alluded to it; he hadn't mentioned that he had been serious about his feelings for that Tejaswini.

"Go on," said Krishna.

"But yes, I stayed committed to Pooja, but at the same time, I kept wondering how it could have been with Tejaswini. But I was with Pooja for three years; your father, on the other hand, was with Prof. Lalita for more than twenty years. I liked Pooja; your father hated a part of his wife's nature. I was with Pooja because I didn't want to hurt her; your father... well, I don't know what the compelling circumstances were."

"We happened to be locked up in the lab for an entire night," said Krishna. "The security guard locked the lab while we were still inside. In my era, that was like a crime..."

Tejaswini looked at her father and then covered her mouth, trying to suppress her giggles. Krishna looked at Anant and smiled awkwardly. A few moments later Tejaswini's giggles stopped.

"So, do you still think, Pooja was murdered?" Anant asked Tejaswini.

"How can you suddenly be so calm about the disappearance of your girlfriend? Don't you feel any pain?"

"I miss Pooja already- her face and all. But the fact is though I have lost my girlfriend, it is only about my relationship status- I am single now. The girl who was my girlfriend and also the girl who I liked, both still exist."

Tejaswini looked at Anant and then glanced at her father. No one reacted.

"And," added Anant, "both the girls had happened to like me."

"Shut up!" Tejaswini said to Anant, barely opening her mouth- almost like Pooja used to do at times.

"I didn't hear you," said Krishna and laughed.

Some other place: Some Other Time:

After the experiment was over, Krishna was relieved that his day with the haughty Lalita was finally over. But the fact was she hadn't spoken to him much except that was absolutely necessary for the sake of the experiment. Krishna looked at her. Maybe she wasn't as bad as he thought she was. But she was surely arrogant.

As he left the college, Krishna felt the weight of the envelope in his pocket- that note from a well-wisher.

Next day, Krishna waited outside the classroom where Supriya was giving her lecture. The bell rang after a while, and she came out. She saw him, and self-consciously nodded at him.

"I wanted to speak to you," he said when she was close enough.

She nodded again.

"I would like it if you go out with me on a date," Krishna said.

Supriya's mouth fell open. She closed it a moment later. She didn't know what to say.

"Er...," she finally uttered. "Er... you know I am older than you?"

"Should it matter? Does it matter?"

"Doesn't it?"

"Oh. I am so sorry that I asked you out, auntie."

"What? Don't call me auntie."

"Why? Aren't you older than me?"

"Just three years," she said.

"Oh. So you mean I am like a younger brother to you?"

"Noooo... Shut up!"

Krishna smiled.

"Come on a date with me," he said again.

"OK. Yes. I will. In fact, I would love to," she smiled and left, totally embarrassed, yet very happy.

VII

The Common Reality:

Two months had passed since the day Anant, Krishna and Tejaswini had had that discussion-cum-argument at home. Tejaswini and Anant now considered each other friends, but she was reluctant to jump into a relationship with him. She had liked him for so long, but after that day, she could no longer look at him the way she did earlier. She liked him even now, but something was missing. Anant had received those vibes from her and he had abstained from trying to convince her that they were meant to take their friendship to the next level. Probably, it was early, he thought. But deep down, he knew it was already quite late. For three years, they had liked each other, and yet hadn't even talked to each other. And now when they talked to each other, she didn't seem to want him as her boyfriend. He knew what it was. It was the time-travel thing that had got in the way. Anant remembered his conversation with the Tejaswini of his original reality. When they had talked to each other on the last day of their exam, she had said that she hoped their paths would cross again in future. Now, in this reality, their path crossed, but nothing seemed to be materialising out of it.

The day when the three of them had talked sitting in the hall of Krishna's apartment, that same day, Krishna had shown his space-time-machine to his daughter and Anant. Tejaswini had a look of dread on her face as she saw it. She was never going to try it out. Obviously, no one was going to allow her to do that. Even Anant and Krishna weren't going to use their own time-machines. They had come to know how a small change could have magnified effects on the future. Krishna had been lucky to get what he wanted, but that wouldn't have got manifested if Anant in another reality hadn't used it to change a minor event of the past. That change in the event had stopped Pooja from being Anant's girlfriend and that had led to the experiment being performed on Krishna himself. So now both Krishna and Anant felt it would be wise to stay away from the machine henceforth. Anant though, at the moment, admired Krishna's machine. It looked plush. The basic scientific principle to travel through space and through time wasn't any different from the one used in Anant's machine, but because Krishna had the liberty of money at his disposal, he had built his machine artistically without having to curtail the cost. After Anant went home that day, a while later, Supriya returned home from college. And Tejaswini didn't waste a single minute before she told her mother about how her father had married her mother. Obviously, Supriya found it all unbelievable until Krishna showed her the machine.

Since that day, Krishna had to face some ire from both Supriya and Tejaswini. Both understood him, both understood why he had done what he did, but both thought it was a bit heartless. How could he have done that when he had known changing the past would wipe out Pooja's existence? In his defence, he said that Pooja didn't disappear. He said that if Pooja was his daughter in one reality, his daughter in any other reality was the same as Pooja. But both Tejaswini and Supriya couldn't reconcile with this logic. Supriya said that if his logic were true, it could be applicable to all situations, and it was not true in Lalita's case. Lalita couldn't say that a daughter in one reality was the same as having a son in the other.

"Gender doesn't matter," Krishna argued.

"No, it doesn't, but if Tejaswini is Pooja, then what should Lalita call her son. She won't be able to say that her son too is Pooja. Because if our Tejaswini is Pooja, how can her son too be Pooja?"

"Agreed, but Tejaswini and Pooja merged. Their souls merged- even their bodies merged to give birth to our Tejaswini. And then if two persons merged and became one, there was space for another person in this reality. That person is Lalita's son."

"What kind of logic is that? Are you playing musical chairs?!" said Supriya, annoyed.

"See, the fact is Tejaswini and Pooja both exist in this reality as one person. That is what should matter."

"You didn't know they would merge when you changed the past. And you didn't know that till Anant came and told you that that was what happened. And though it seems it happened, it is just a perspective. It is not an undebatable fact."

"I changed the past thinking whoever my child would be, he or she would be the same as Pooja."

"No, you didn't. If you had thought so, after coming back to your timeline, you wouldn't have checked what happened to Lalita and whether she had a daughter. You found out about her, but you hadn't tried to find out about me and my daughter in your original reality. I know this because you said you didn't know Tejaswini in both realities looked the same. You didn't care. You just wanted me, even if that meant you could lose your daughter from that reality."

Krishna had lost the argument. What he meant was that he would love any child of his as he had loved Pooja, but he didn't say that. He had indeed lost the argument, and Supriya was right. He had wanted her at any cost. Pooja was his daughter, but she was also Lalita's daughter. He wanted to have a child that was his and Supriya's. Yes, it had been heartless.

The same had happened with Anant. Tejaswini considered him a friend, and she did so because she thought he had been committed to Pooja and that he had not changed his reality to get rid of Pooja. Whatever he had changed, he had done that unwittingly. But he had supported her father, and he seemed to have taken the loss of Pooja not very seriously. She knew he saw Tejaswini as a merging of two persons, but she suspected he liked her because of her physical appearance rather than her mind. Anant too somewhat appeared to her as heartless though not as heartless as her own father. She loved her father and she liked Anant, but what they had done or what logic they found solace in, that seemed heartless. Because both Supriya and Tejaswini thought that Krishna and Anant were more or less heartless, both men now suffered. Krishna knew Tejaswini had refrained herself from having a relationship with Anant and he blamed himself for that. Anant, on the other hand, thought he should have directly talked to Krishna without involving Tejaswini. But he had involved her and now if she was keeping herself away even from Anant, he knew Krishna would be suffering a lot more from this cold treatment, and not just from his daughter. Anant had liked Krishna in the previous reality and he liked him even now. He had liked Pooja and he missed her, but he knew his logic was impeccable. He knew Pooja and Tejaswini were the same person in this reality. So, missing Pooja was not logical. Pooja was Pooja because of her father, not her mother. And Tejaswini of the original reality too was Tejaswini mostly because of her mother. The Tejaswini of the current reality had the traits of both these persons. She was Pooja, and she was Tejaswini. How was he ever going to convince her? He wasn't heartless. He had only accepted his reality. He missed Pooja and also that Tejaswini from that reality, but both these persons were in front of him; he in fact missed not those two persons from that reality- he missed that reality itself; it made him feel nostalgic to think about that reality which now seemed better than the current one.

VIII

The Tweak:

Tejaswini hadn't come to college that day. She hadn't sent Anant a message about her absence. Well, she wasn't his girlfriend, and he didn't expect her to tell him everything, but he was worried. But he didn't call her. He didn't want her to feel he was trying to get too close to her. So, he carried on with his day at the college. Finally, it was over, and as he came out of the college, he was looking forward to tomorrow, hoping to see her the next day. He was walking home alone, when he was startled by a tap on his shoulder. He turned to find Tejaswini's father in front of him.

"We need to talk," they both said at the same time, and then they both smiled.

Tejaswini had been right. They were indeed like each other, and now with the same kind of data uploaded in their brains, they were even more so. Both had asked for physics and chemistry uploads in their brains in two different realities. And after the upload, both had eventually got hooked to the idea of time, and then had invented the space-time-machine. Moreover, now they were suffering because of the similar cold treatment meted out to them by the persons they loved.

"Where is Tejaswini? She didn't come to college today."

"She has a cold, and it is convenient for me that she stayed home. That way, I could come here."

"Are you thinking on the same lines as I am?" Anant asked Krishna.

Krishna lifted up his hand to show him a bag. Anant smiled slightly and nodded.

"But yes, we have to discuss this first," Krishna said.

"Yes. Should I get mine too?"

"Yes."

Krishna and Anant walked towards the latter's home. They didn't talk or discuss as neither wanted a break in their discussion when Anant went home. Krishna stayed back at the mouth of the lane as Anant went home, kept his college bag, made an excuse at home about going out with a friend, and carried his inconspicuous bag of the space-time-machine back to where Krishna was waiting for him.

"OK," said Krishna. "First, the plan."

"We go back in time. You pose as the father of Tejaswini..."

"Pose?" Krishna interrupted Anant. "I *am* her father."

"Oh yes. This multiple-reality thing is sometimes confusing. I am so much used to the reality in which you were Pooja's father that... Well, you are Tejaswini's father. So you go and tell my younger self to express my feelings to her. When it comes from you, the younger me will talk to her. She was interested in me; so when the younger me talks to her, she will hopefully become my girlfriend and then..."

"And then all the unwanted things from the last couple of months erase themselves, and a third reality is formed."

"But are we correct, or are we missing something?" asked Anant. "I want to be sure as I don't want a totally absurd third reality to form. We are already facing the effects of our time-travel."

"OK," agreed Krishna. "We shall think aloud. I tell the younger Anant to express his feelings to Tejaswini. He does that, and here we assume that Tejaswini now becomes the younger Anant's girlfriend. We are already back to our timeline. The effect is instantaneous for us when we return here. When we come back, we will still remember all this, that is, you will remember your original reality, I will remember mine, and we will both remember our current reality, which is the second reality for both of us, but apart from those two sets of memories, we will also have a third set of memories, and that will be of the third reality that replaces this current reality. In it, you are already Tejaswini's boyfriend. But one fine day, two months back, you will remember all about Pooja. With that, you will also come to know that Pooja's and Tejaswini's father are one and the same because I would have already met you once as Tejaswini's father. You will have the knowledge of time-travel and you will decipher that I too might have used something like that when I ushered you towards Tejaswini. Or even if you don't have all the answers, you may at least directly approach me instead of involving Tejaswini."

"No, wait," said Anant. "I don't think the younger me will remember about Pooja two months back because if we time-travel now, we would have changed the reality and then there would not be a you or a me who has been in the time-loop two months back. In this third reality, we would have created a time-loop at this moment, and I think, until today, you or me will not have any memories of the other realities. But when our past-selves reach this point in time, suddenly we will have the memories of our respective original realities, this current reality and the third reality as well. We also won't have our space-time-machines till today."

"Hmmm...," Krishna was thinking. "I guess you are right, but if you are right then we have a problem."

"What problem?"

"Say, we use our machines now. We go to the past, and return exactly at this spot. Until we return, the you and the me of this third reality will have no idea that they are time-travellers. You might be at your home and I might be at the institute. What happens to them when we return here? See; we will be explicitly programming our machines to bring us here. So we will override the natural space coordinates. And that means when we return here, the you and me from the third reality will vanish from their current spots and teleport here and merge with us. That is not a problem for us. We will know through our memories what happened, but imagine that you at your home while talking to your parents suddenly vanish from front of their eyes."

Anant thought about it. Krishna was correct. That would happen. But why hadn't such a thing happened in their first time-travel? It would have but Anant was at home at night and his parents were asleep, and he was now guessing that Krishna too must have done something like that.

"Yes, you are right," Anant said to Krishna. "But then how do we do it?"

"I don't know. But we will discuss further and come to this part later."

"OK. I have one more doubt. When we go back to the past now, can't you directly tell the younger me that you are from the future?"

"I don't think so. And I think you too have reservations against doing such a thing."

"Yes. Far too much knowledge about the future need not be disclosed."

"Correct," said Krishna. "And then when your past-self gets to today through the natural passage of time, he will know for sure how it all happened."

"Now you could have done this all by yourself, but you didn't. You involved me and I am grateful to you for that."

"I have to involve you. First of all, you supported me in front of my daughter," said Krishna. "Moreover, if I don't involve you and we don't make the journey into the past and back here together, only I will remember how the third reality came into existence. I don't want that to happen. Also, on the basis of what we discussed just now, if I went alone, you will no longer have your database in your brain because you will not be in the time-loop."

"Oh! Oh! Yes, you are right," Anant agreed. "So, I just become a normal human being that I was. Now, I am even more grateful to you."

"You need not be. I hadn't thought about it. You know I had my speculations wrong until you pointed that out."

"Good that neither of us made a decision to travel alone."

"In fact," said Krishna, "we did that earlier. But you with your machine and memories got saved at that time perhaps because you were inside the time-loop when I changed my reality."

"Yes, you are right. And that just happens to be a very fortunate coincidence for me." said Anant.

"So coming back to what we left pending- how do we prevent the you and me from the third reality from vanishing in front of people's eyes?"

"We do it at night from our homes at the same time?" suggested Anant.

"OK. Tell me if you have a specific date in mind."

"In fact, yes. In my second year in the current reality, I had missed all lectures and was waiting outside the college, contemplating on whether to approach Tejaswini. It was Rose Day in our college, and I was in two minds. In the end, I couldn't gather the courage..."

Krishna asked him the date and the time and Anant told him.

"Would I be risking being seen by Tejaswini?" asked Krishna.

"No. She was inside the college the entire time, and I hope she was hoping that I would give her a rose and a card."

"Fine then we will go there at night," said Krishna.

"Wait," said Anant.

"What happened?"

"We should be able to do it together."

"We *will be* doing it together."

"No. I mean we should leave to the past at exactly the same time. We should also return here together. If we make the time-travel individually, there will be a difference at which we press the buttons on our machines.

Even if the difference is infinitesimally small, there will still be a difference and..."

"And this will lead to the creation of one more reality," Krishna completed Anant's statement. These two realities may be very similar, but not exactly the same. They will merge, but still we don't want a fourth reality to get created when it can be avoided. And we obviously don't want one of us to lose the data uploaded in our brain. By the way, that was brilliant of you."

"Thank you, but how do we do it- how do we travel together?" asked Anant.

"Er... Do you have an extra USB cable?"

"Not an extra one, but I can disconnect one of the batteries."

"Will your machine work without one of the batteries?"

"Yes."

"Then, give that cable to me."

Anant disconnected a battery and handed over a cable to Krishna. He connected the two time machines with this cable and made some adjustments on the dials of his machine.

"That should do it," Krishna said. "I am now overriding your control on your machine."

"You had already had that facility inbuilt?"

"An added feature to connect an extra device. I don't have your feature though- the automatic timer setting."

Anant smiled.

"So now, we will have to physically meet each other to join our machines together," he said.

"Yes," said Krishna, "but that isn't much of a challenge. Both our machines are built to teleport. I will teleport here at night. You do the same. As long as we do not use the time-travel feature of our machines, we won't be creating a new reality. After we meet here, we will join our machines and go to the past together."

Anant took Krishna to a secluded spot behind the last of the many lanes in this locality and told him that they would teleport here at night.

At night, Anant and Krishna met at the decided spot at the decided time. Krishna joined the machines and set the time. In a moment, they were gone.

Two Years into the Past:

Anant and Krishna conjured up in the empty staircase of the college. They both got out of their suits. Anant waited on the stairs with both their machines while Krishna went out to see the younger Anant.

"Hi," Krishna said. "You must be Anant."

"Yes," said the younger Anant. "But I didn't recognise you."

"I am Krishna Sathe."

"Sathe?"

"Yes. That surname, I am sure, will make you think of only one person."

"Huh?"

"I am her father- the girl about whom you are thinking of right now."

"Huh?" Anant's reaction again was just an exclamation.

"Go and talk to her. She must be waiting for you. It's Rose Day, I heard."

"But..."

"Why are you making one-worded noises?"

"Er..."

"There you go again."

Anant smiled.

"Don't tell her I told you anything. Promise me."

"Yes, I won't tell her anything. But you don't even know me."

"She knows you. That's enough for me. Go. She too thinks about you the way you think about her."

"I don't think... Did she tell you that?"

"Not directly. But then how do you think I know about you? Will you go now and tell her what you feel for her, or should I go on a date with you?"

"No. No," Anant smiled. "I will go. But how did you know where to find me?"

Krishna frowned at Anant.

"OK. OK," Anant took the cue. "I will go and try to tell her that..."

"Try?" Krishna exclaimed.

"I will. I *will*."

Anant disappeared into the college.

The Tweak (continued...):

Krishna and Anant were back in their own timeline, but now in a different reality- the third reality for the both of them. As memories flooded in, they were overwhelmed, but it wasn't as bad as the first time-travel for both of them. This time, it was just two years into the past, and moreover, not much had changed except that both remembered an upcoming event.

"Oh no," said Anant.

"Oh no," said Krishna.

"I have to be at your place tomorrow with my parents."

"And I have to be at mine to greet you."

"But what was the urgency? Tejaswini and I still haven't completed our post-graduation."

"You are not getting engaged. This is just an informal meeting," said Krishna.

"So, it was your idea? To rush these things?"

Krishna coughed.

"We better call it a night," said Krishna.

"Yeah. Yeah."

Neither Anant nor Tejaswini had gone to college today. Though Anant had memories of him being Tejaswini's boyfriend for the past two years or so, when he saw her today, it felt like he was meeting his girlfriend for the first time. If his brain were to be divided into three parts for three realities, then two parts of his brain were meeting Tejaswini as his girlfriend for the first time. In the light of the three sets of memories that he had, he knew this was one of the happiest moments of his life.

Supriya sat beside Krishna. She looked very beautiful, and she smiled at her guests and talked to them politely, and Anant felt that if he hadn't supported Krishna earlier, he would have done it today, for Supriya and Lalita were classes apart. Anant was supposed to be meeting them for the first time. Krishna knew this, and when he shook hands with Anant formally, he winked at him.

"Is the machine safe?" Anant whispered to Krishna while Tejaswini, Supriya and Anant's parents were busy talking to one another.

"Yes."

"And all's good? No one remembers anything, right?"

"No. That's what we did. We changed it. You are just getting anxious. Don't worry."

"I was just asking to be sure whether there were any memories..."

"No. All's good," Krishna assured him and then added in a boisterous manner, directing a question at Anant, "So how did you two meet? Tejaswini's too shy to tell me that."

Anant gave a knowing look to Krishna.

"It began on a day called the Rose Day..."

"But it had started much before that," said Tejaswini and blushed instantly.

Epilogue

"How could you completely forget about it?" Krishna asked Anant.

"How can a thing that has still not happened be forgotten?"

"Shut up! Don't give that time-travel cause-effect crap. We are both well-versed with it. It's all your mistake."

"My mistake? You are the one supposed to be working at the institute."

Krishna had called up Anant, and asked him to meet at the secluded spot near Anant's home. Anant had not gone to the college yet, and Krishna had met him on his way to the institute.

"It's all because you are so smitten by Tejaswini."

"Hahaha... Is it because of me smitten by Tejaswini or you smitten by... Come on, don't make me say it. It's weird to talk on this subject to my to-be father-in-law about my to-be mother-in-law."

"That's what? How dare you?" Krishna said in mock anger and Anant laughed.

"But seriously, how could you miss this...?" Anant said.

"You also didn't think about it, did you?"

"No, but you work there and see Prof. Wagh..."

"I don't happen to see him daily. Moreover, in both realities- your original and my original ones- this happened much before now. That's the reason we are in this current third reality. And in my original reality, I had come to know about it a month before it was actually going to happen. Wagh had wanted me to be the subject, but this time, he didn't even ask me. I came to know only today. Imagine, coming to know of something in your own institute through the newspapers."

"Any idea why they are looking for the candidates this late?"

"Maybe because I joined the institute late in this reality," replied Krishna. "In that reality in which Lalita was my wife I had joined the institute only after one year at college as a professor. But, in the second reality- and this remains unchanged in the current reality as well- I got married to Supriya and I stayed at the college a little longer. There was a delay of two years before I joined the institute. As a result, Wagh, who was my find, joined our institute much later than in my original reality. This might have been the reason that this test got delayed in the current reality. And because of the difficult circumstances that we were going through in our personal lives and then in us being happy at our nullifying them, we totally forgot about the main thing that gave us our powers. We can still appear for the test, and get selected. That way..."

"That way our brain will be uploaded with the same database we already have. That won't do us any good. What if our brain bursts?"

"What? Our brain is a balloon or what?" Krishna said and laughed.

"Stop joking. I didn't mean it literally. So what should we do now?"

"It appears like a madman forgot something in a story he wrote and then added it as an epilogue."

"Exactly. Prof. Wagh's invention led to all this mess- well, it wasn't exactly a mess- and then after the happy ending we thought it was, there comes this epilogue with a climax. Except that there is no madman here other than the one who forgot what's going on in his own institute."

"Or the madman who forgot that if Wagh's invention is used on someone else, it may backfire on us," Krishna retorted. "If someone else builds a time-machine and reality changes for us, we won't even know what changed. We may longer have the database in our heads, no time-machines, nothing. Perhaps no Supriya, no Tejaswini. I don't want to get stuck with Lalita again."

"Uh-oh!"

"What happened?"

"Tejaswini just texted me saying she read the ad, and she is going to give it a try."

"She will get selected. She has all it requires," Krishna said.

"And she will be able to build a time-machine."

"We don't want that to happen. She's my daughter. But still, we can't have anyone else build a time-machine. No one in this reality knows about our super brains or the time-machines. Let it be that way. If someone else has this super power, it will be a mess."

"I agree."

"So what's the plan?" asked Krishna.

"I don't have a plan."

"We cannot nullify Wagh's invention through time-travel. It's his life's work. At least for the past seven years, he has been working on this project."

"So, how are we supposed to put a stop to this? By the way, I haven't received the incentive money your institute promised me in my original reality."

Krishna slapped his head as Anant laughed.

"It's after two years, have you forgotten that? Or was it different in your reality?"

"No, it was the same. But since they won't be working on my brain in this reality, I suppose I won't receive it."

"Stop worrying about the incentive; the experiment has made you so talented that you can open such an institute yourself and start paying incentives to others."

"Hmmm... I hope one day it will be so. Even you can do it."

"Yes, but my doing it doesn't matter. You are young."

"But you can buy your own institute."

"And if we can do it..."

"Yes," said Anant, "we will be able to control the outcome of the experiment."

"But then owning the institute is still in the future. None of us are millionaires at this moment. So when we become that rich, we will have to go back in time and nullify..."

"What?" said Anant, "you are already counting your chickens, and the eggs have not even been laid yet. You just got carried away. First of all, even if we become rich, we can't bring future money to the past. And by the time we own your institute, there is a high probability that someone else might have built a time-machine, and we would have lost all our powers."

"You are right. We are back to square one. What can we do now? It seems to me we will have to postpone our decision to do something about it until we have an idea."

"But," said Anant, "we should really get to the task of thinking because it is just a week before the test."

"That is fine," said Krishna. "We can always come back in time and nullify the test or stop the ad from going to the newspapers. We can do that even now, but that's a temporary and a desperate solution. And we still have to figure out how to do it, but our brains will manage to think about something; I am sure," Krishna paused and then added, "Even if they find a suitable candidate, he or she is not going to build a time-machine instantly. Moreover, there will be some days after the candidate is selected and before the experiment is performed on his or her brain. So we have some time. But I don't want any temporary solution. I want a permanent one. So yes, let's start thinking."

Anant and Krishna were about to leave when Krishna suddenly froze.

"Oh crap!" he said.

"What happened?" asked Anant.

"How did she know we are here?"

"Who?" asked Anant and turned to look in the direction where Krishna was looking.

"She must have followed you," said Krishna.

"How could she have followed me? I came here directly from home; she must have followed *you*," Anant said as he watched Tejaswini walking up towards them.

Neither of them moved. They didn't know what to do. They just stood there like statues.

"What should we say?" asked Krishna.

"She's your daughter. You decide."

"Hmmm... We came here to discuss the plans for your wedding."

"What? Why are you in such a hurry about that? First you planned that small get-together and now *wedding*! No, she won't buy it."

"OK, then you decide. She is your girlfriend. I am leaving."

"Ha... You are leaving. Try it."

Anant was right. Krishna didn't move even an inch.

"What are you two doing here?" Tejaswini asked as she came and stopped in front of them."

"We can ask you the same question," Krishna and Anant both said at the same time.

"We should stop saying things in chorus," Krishna said to Anant.

"Yes," Anant agreed.

"So, what are you two doing here?" Tejaswini asked again.

"Er...," Anant said.

"What?" said Tejaswini.

"He's thinking," said Krishna to his daughter, "at least give him some time to think of an answer."

"Wow! So you two are going to lie to me."

"We were planning a small get-together," said Krishna. "It was going to be a surprise."

Tejaswini raised her eyebrows, and it meant she wasn't buying it.

"But you didn't tell us what you are doing here," Anant said. "Did you follow your father here? You suspect him of something? Don't you trust your own father?" Anant was trying to embarrass Tejaswini.

"Stop trying that. It's not working," she said.

Anant and Krishna looked at each other. There was no lie good enough that would convince her.

"Oh yes," said Krishna, and that itself gave away the fact that he had just thought about something convincing; Anant winced at his to-be father-in-law's inability to lie.

"I asked him," said Krishna, "to meet here to discuss the test that my institute is conducting. I want him to appear for the test."

"But you never said anything to me about it. You own daughter... I have started wondering whether *he* is your son," Tejaswini said, and Anant remembered Pooja having said the same thing; Tejaswini *is* Pooja, isn't she?- thought Anant.

"Now stop trying to lie, you two," she said. "I know why you are here."

"You know?" again Krishna and Anant said in chorus.

"Really? You two should have been twins. You think the same, you say the same things and you do the same things too."

"What did we do?" asked Anant, and then he and Krishna looked at each other with eyes wide open.

"You couldn't have known we were here...," said Krishna.

"...unless we ourselves told you that," Anant completed Krishna's sentence.

Tejaswini smiled a smug smile.

"And neither of us told you that we are here. So, that means...," Krishna said.

"I hope you have not come here alone," said Anant, horror on his face.

"No," said Krishna. "If we told her, we wouldn't let her come here alone."

"Yes, you are right," Anant said, now relaxing a bit.

"Had your twin-brothers' talk?" Tejaswini said. "But you are right. By the way, I hadn't thought you would decipher that so quickly, and I am impressed. Yes, I am from the future."

"What is 344 by 12.1?" Anant asked.

"28.429752...," Tejaswini and Krishna answered together.

"OK. Stop!" Anant stopped them before they could add more decimal places to the number, and then Anant and Krishna looked at each other again.

They knew Tejaswini too had a database uploaded in her brain.

"So you got selected?"

"Yes, and I too like you two asked for physics and chemistry. Obviously, I was totally oblivious to the fact that you already had the same information in your brains. And then in course of time, I too, like you two built a time-machine. But my father here caught me inventing it, and then you two from my timeline had no choice but to tell me everything."

"And they, I mean, we from the future are here too."

"Yes. How else were we all to remain in the same reality? Our space-time-machines are synchronised."

"We should meet them," Anant suggested.

"No," Krishna objected. "I know that you feel- and even I have also concluded the same at times- that the paradox involving time-travelling and meeting your own self in the past is over-hyped. Reality will mould itself to our whims, I think, but we need not test it unless absolutely necessary."

"Yes," agreed Tejaswini, "that's the reason you two from the future have not come here to meet you."

"So, tell us why you are here," said Anant. "But wait. If you are from the future, how do you know that your father has still not talked to you about Prof. Wagh's experiment?" and then as he said it, both he and Krishna suddenly fear grip them.

They were so surprised to see Tejaswini from the future in front of them that this had not occurred to them even when she mentioned that they had told her everything. If she knew that both of them had built time-machines and both had the database uploaded in their brains, and in her reality she was the only one who was selected for the experiment, then she would also know that they got their brains uploaded with the database in some other reality, and if so, then she would know about Pooja and Lalita. And if she knew that then the tweak that they performed to get into Tejaswini's and Supriya's good books had just become inconsequential. Anant and Krishna together realised all this, but they dared not look at each other.

"Oh, that? You two told me everything," said Tejaswini, and Anant and Krishna had a sinking feeling in their stomachs. "You two from my timeline told me that when I meet you here, my father still hasn't talked to the Tejaswini from this timeline about the experiment. I also know about how Anant had got selected and I hadn't and then when he built the time-machine, he went to confront the ragging group. This led to the formation of a new reality and in this reality, the event when I became his girlfriend got delayed. In this reality because of some other unknown subtle changes, my father chose to get the experiment performed on himself. He invented the time-machine and realised how dangerous it could be if the general public had access to such an invention. So he went back in time to give himself a note that asked his younger self to delay his joining the institute so that Prof. Wagh's recruitment and consequently the experiment would also get delayed. Luckily when he was in the past, Anant from the original reality was in his time-loop too, and when that Anant from his original reality merged with Anant of the second reality, he had this database in his brain. He now also had his time-machine with him. But though the event of the experiment got delayed in this newest reality, you still didn't have any idea to stop it and so I too in the end became a part of your league."

Anant and Krishna now actually looked at each other. They from the future had told Tejaswini almost the entire truth just leaving Pooja and Lalita out of the story. Phew! That was close.

"OK, good. Very good. So, now tell us why you are here." Anant repeated his original question.

"As I said your meeting here wasn't a success. You still don't have any idea how you are going to stop Prof. Wagh's experiment. You also had no idea in the reality that I come from, and that's the reason the test was conducted and I got selected. I asked for physics and chemistry as the preferred subjects to be uploaded in my brain. And then I built the time-machine. Luckily for you two and yes, admittedly for me too, there was no other candidate who got selected. So the experiment was performed only on me. But, after two years, when they find out everything's fine with me, they may start performing it on some volunteers, and those volunteers need not pass the test too. If all goes well with them, they may then start performing the upload on a commercial level. But this has to stop right here, as we cannot have too many time-machines. Obviously, not all will build time-machines. Doing that not only depends on the database uploaded, but also on the intelligence of the candidate. We three did it; that does not necessarily mean that all people who undergo the data upload will be able to do it. But it also does not mean that they won't be able to do it. So, basically, we have to stop the experiment from going commercial. You have to take over the institute. So here are some numbers," Tejaswini handed over an envelope to Anant and Krishna.

"Those are lottery numbers. Different lotteries spaced over time. Not very huge amounts- huge but not very huge when considered individually- but the cumulative amounts for both of you over the next two years will be enough to buy more than fifty percent shares of the institute. Once that happens, you can control the experiment from within and without having to time-travel and risk changing realities. You have two more years. So don't worry."

"So you are from two years into the future?" said Anant.

"Yes, my final follow-up visit to the institute is pending. After that, some more people will be tested with the experiment. You have to stop that. When I return to my timeline, we will already have control over the institute. Thereafter, even if the experiment is performed on others, we would have a say in the kind of data that is uploaded in the brains of those people. Best of luck."

"Yes, luck is required to win lotteries," Krishna smiled.

"What about the people who have won those lotteries? If we win them now, then we would be stripping them of their winning amounts," said Anant.

"Yes, you said the same thing in the future."

"Oh yes, I forget it's us there too."

"Don't worry about the other winners; we have selected only those lotteries where there wasn't a jackpot winner, but now there will be."

"We had suspected that you would be selected for the experiment," said Krishna.

"Thank you," Tejaswini said, "for believing in my brain. And that's the best part of time-travel that even if I change something in the past, my memories remain intact. So I will have this data at my disposal forever, unless someone else changes the reality and we remain outside the time-loop."

"Yes," said Anant. "We will not let that happen. We are now the protectors of the time-loop."

The three of them smiled, and Tejaswini now walked away.

When Tejaswini from the future along with Anant and Krishna from the same timeline returned to their present, they were already rich and owned more than half of the shares of the institute. Prof. Wagh's experiment continued, but Krishna, Anant and Tejaswini had a huge say on whom it could be conducted, and they had also deleted chunks of physics from the database. The three of them continued to work together for the betterment of the human race through scientific experiments born out of their ideas, but they remained possessive about the time-loop. And if ever they would feel their reality was in danger, they would go together and tweak the past.

Printed by Libri Plureos GmbH in Hamburg,
Germany